ALL THE VOICES CRY

ALICE
PETERSEN

ALL THE
VOICES CRY

STORIES

BIBLIOASIS

FIRST EDITION

Library and Archives Canada Cataloguing in Publication

Petersen, Alice, 1970-
    All the voices cry / Alice Petersen.

Short stories.
ISBN 978-1-926845-52-4

    I. Title.

PS8631.E825A45 2012   C813'.6   C2011-907875-9

Biblioasis acknowledges the ongoing financial support of the Government of Canada through the Canada Council for the Arts, Canadian Heritage, the Canada Book Fund; and the Government of Ontario through the Ontario Arts Council.

PRINTED AND BOUND IN CANADA

Contents

After Summer

JAKE AND I GREW up without a mother, which wasn't that bad, although we ate a lot of boiled peas. Back when we were kids, before Valmae came into the picture, Dad rented a boathouse every year for the whole of August, up at Lac Perdu, near Shawinigan. He spent the summer months growing a fat Hemingway moustache while the sun darkened his shoulders to the colour of beer. We weren't supposed to sleep at the boathouse, but in early August, when the concrete city had baked hard in the sun, Dad would drive us up to the lake on Friday nights. We'd light citronella candles to keep the mosquitoes off, eat rubbery pizza and drink warm juice out of the cooler. When the bats came out we'd go up into the woods to pee before going to sleep in a row on the boathouse floor, listening to the water lapping and Dad breathing in the dark.

On Saturday mornings Dad sat in the boathouse attic typing up the poems that he carried in his head during the rest of the year. The poems were mainly about women once glimpsed through panes of frosted glass, because he was a mail carrier with two kids and that's about as close as he ever got. If you stood at the bottom of the ladder to the attic you could hear Dad up there groaning over lines about galoshes and garden paths, white terriers and white negligees, the day-long ning-nong of the bell and the endless wait for a snug fit in scented flesh.

While Dad worked at his poems, Jake and I squatted on the dock making fat duck-farting noises by blowing through blades of grass. Sometimes we would stir the water with sticks, or catch horseflies and hand-deliver them into the webs of spiders. Dad was in his confessional and we were being mostly good. Eventually Dad would climb back down the ladder, his skin smelling of hot pine boards and the edgy stench of the bats that lived behind the rafters, and then we would all swing off the rope on the tree and drop into the water.

I have this vision of Dad at the lake during the long summers, emerging from the waves, his chest hair plastered into dripping points. Shaggy Dad, Poseidon Dad, ever-strong Dad, and Jake and I screaming and clinging to him like monkeys while he dunked us up and down. And eventually he would say, "Clear off, I feel a poem coming on," and he would grab a couple of beers out of the cooler dug into the shallows and disappear up the ladder into the attic to write, while we sidled off to the cliffs to look for fossils.

Once we didn't clear off. Instead we dragged a ladder out of the grass and propped it up against the boathouse wall. Jake was just peering into the window at the top when a rotten rung of the ladder gave way and he fell and knocked himself out.

"Dad's got no clothes on and he's crying," he said when he woke up, by which time Dad was fully dressed and driving us into town as fast as he could.

It hadn't occurred to us that Dad might be unhappy because we weren't, and it was summertime, and Dad was just Dad. We knew he drank at night on the boathouse steps; the more beer he drank, the more bottles there were to get a refund on.

Just after we turned fourteen, Dad started dating Valmae, and that was the end of summers at the lake, because there was no plug at the boathouse for her hair dryer. Valmae was a secretary at our high school. She took it on to rescue Dad from the two giant squid choking him in their tentacled embrace. First she moved in and began cooking balanced meals, which in itself wasn't a bad thing, but then she persuaded Dad to give up mail delivery and open a dry-cleaning business. There was an office out back of the store where Valmae talked on the phone to tardy clients, threatening to send their suits and dresses to Colombia in a container ship if they did not come to collect them. *Most companies don't bother to phone,* she would say. My father pressed the trousers. The heat made his hair damp and curled it behind his ears. I worked the cash after school. I liked the punking noise the receipts made when you stuck them on the spike. Jake refused to have anything to do with it.

A couple of years after Dad hooked up with Valmae, Jake slipped the net and hitchhiked to Big Sur. Four years passed and Valmae spotted him on a home-renovating show, making a plywood stereo cabinet on a suburban front lawn, satisfying women across North America with the kerthunk of his nail gun and the hiss and judder of the compressor. He was giving the camera his long, lazy grin and he had his ball cap at a howdy-pardner tilt. The dentist always said that Jake had too many teeth, but he had enough for television.

After Jake lit out I stayed on, typing out my angst one finger at a time on Dad's Olivetti in awful, badly spaced rhyming verse about hideous misunderstandings and imagined perfect communion. After I had written each poem, I would shred it and let my geriatric gerbils make a nest of my thoughts.

I haven't spent my life looking for a mother, and I certainly haven't looked for one in Valmae. Valmae keeps her hair pretty. She sews sofa cushions. She is a wreath-of-dried-flowers-with-seasonal-bear-on-the-front-door kind of person. I haven't missed being mothered, but I'm kind of missing Dad. Valmae has him cornered like a bull, down on his Hemingway knees, helpless beneath the weight of house and car payments. Every day he's slapped by the coats on the electric rack at the dry cleaner's as they flare out and twirl around the corner. But he seems happy. I have to be honest about that. Maybe Dad has a good time between Valmae's satin sheets.

The other weekend I went out to buy a chair just like the one Dad used to sit on to write his poetry. Dad's chair had a woven seat made of some kind of hide, thick and yellow like old cooked pasta. We always thought of it as catgut since Dad emitted such excruciating yowls during his bouts of work. The chair had no screws in it—just wooden plugs, and when Dad stretched back, the chair creaked from the hip joint. Not a comfortable chair, but a speaking chair that moaned along with Dad's efforts to express himself. Of course we had to leave it behind in the boathouse with all the other stuff that was never ours.

I drove out across the plain toward St. Antoine, thinking of the time when it had been boreal forest, and how the rustling leaves must have roared in the wind, like the sea in the fall. My dog had her head out the passenger window. Flecks of saliva whipped off her tongue and stuck to the rear door. There never was a dog with so much saliva, or such perpetual anticipation of the good to come.

The antique store was a real barn of a place, hung with moose heads and ancient egg beaters and leather pouches of oxidizing fish-hooks. Most of the furniture had been scraped and repainted, as if the years had not given it enough story, so story had to be added to it.

I asked about chairs and was directed upstairs to a stifling room under the rafters, filled with golden light that came through panels let into the ceiling. At one end were stacks of tables—end tables, side tables with barley-twist legs, dining-room tables, bedside tables with drawers, washstands—so many surfaces for putting down cups, saucers, books, typewriters and beer bottles. And there were hundreds of chairs spooning into each other: battered, scraped, loose-bottomed, straw-filled, hidebound chairs, which meant that there were also hundreds of lapsed poets, hundreds of adult children looking for lost fathers, and hundreds of family stories about stepmothers, which, when it came down to it, might not be so different one from another. The weight of all those chairs hanging among the rafters filled me with panic.

After Valmae came, there was none of the tangy essence of bat left about my father. The moist air of dry cleaning softened Dad's poems and turned them to powdery mould. And now Dad's going to marry Valmae, and after I've signed him over as a going concern I wonder when I'll be talking to him again, because it's his life now, and he's chosen to live like that, with her and her dried flowers. I just wish that Jake would slouch on in with his arms crossed over his chest and smile in his lazy summer-dog way, because I really want to take him out for a beer and ask him if he thinks that we somehow made Dad feel smothered when we clung on to him. I mean, when he dunked us in the water, did he ever wish that he could let us go? And now that we are twenty, has he at last let us go? And if he has, what is it like to tread water alone, without even a chair to hold onto when the spring floods come?

Among the Trees

WHAT REMAINED OF Hugh had been delivered to Jan in a corrugated cardboard box, marked Temporary Container. Jan knew that Hugh would have been delighted, he would have positively roared with laughter at the aptness of the label, given that he had made it his life's work to celebrate the passing of time. She held the box with both hands while she made her way uphill through the bare forest, her coat snagging on the dead branches of fallen spruce. Eventually she arrived at a high rock where the cliff fell away towards the lake in a jumble of boulders and moss and clinging cedars. Across the lake chilly banks of cloud lay along the hills, and the birches stood arrayed in white stripes against the cocoa brown and blue of the land. It was as good a place as any to do the scattering.

She opened the box for the first time and looked doubtfully at the granular presence in the plastic bag. It was not Hugh in that box. Hugh would never have had anything to do with a plastic bag, or a twist tie. Hugh was already out mingling with the other molecules in the air. He had always been everywhere and nowhere in particular.

Time to scatter, and she saw herself walking behind a plough, flinging seed in wide arcs. She could hear his gravelly voice, *It may be the most useful work of art I ever create. Ashes are good for plants. Here darling,* she said to him internally, *try arranging this.* She flung them out of the bag and they fell over the cliff edge not in a poetic swirl, but in a pattering shower like a fall of drops from a tree long after the rain has passed.

Jan had been twenty-two when she inherited the antique log cabin on the edge of the great forest of the Mauricie. Her grandparents, tweedy Anglican folk with quiet voices and expensive shoes, had recognized that Jan alone of all the Toronto clan would not immediately sell the fishing camp at Lac Perdu in exchange for a manicured rock in Georgian Bay. There had been no animosity in the family when the bequest was revealed. As Hugh put it, Jan's family was territorially gifted, and there were enough properties of one kind or another to keep all the descendants happy.

Built by wealthy Americans in the late nineteenth century, the cedar-lined interior of the cabin had acquired a rich patina through repeated suffusions of sunlight, wood smoke and evening tobacco. Jan had studied albums of minute snapshots of men and women in knickerbockers posing with their catches, while narrow-eyed local guides crouched in the background, sleeves rolled up to expose their hard, sun-darkened forearms. Jan had an interest in photography and an interest in history, and now she had inherited enough money to indulge in both.

About this time Hugh found Jan in the way a very young woman sometimes dreams of being found and trapped under the hot spotlight of a powerful regard. The art gallery had been full, the people arranged in small clusters in front of the paintings, gesturing with their wine glasses, some ignoring the paintings altogether and living only for the subtle readjustment of the room as each new person entered it. Jan was wearing the ruby silk that she had cut on the grain and the fabric swirled over her thighs. She feigned indifference to the stocky figure with his shorn white hair bristling like filaments, but at any time during the evening she could have told you exactly where "Hugh-the-sculptor" was to be found. A day later, a chance meeting at the liquor store and three bottles of Chilean red wine resulted in hours and whole days in bed and out of it, as their two bodies locked together and tumbled again and again off a high cliff into the warm air. Jan's life could not be the same afterwards. Hugh made the idea of answering the telephone in an art gallery seem like ridiculous work. Jan resigned from the job and began to take her photography seriously. She took Hugh off to spend the summer in the cabin in the woods.

At the beginning a great crowd of friends visited the cabin. Seated in a protective ring of citronella candles they ate berry compote off leaves and argued late into the night. When the mosquitoes became unbearable, they stripped and swam out along the drunken path of the moon. They were a mixed bunch, all happy to escape Toronto. Vernon Hasp, the film maker, and his girlfriend, Tiny, made the long drive across to Quebec in a convertible. Tiny brought bowls of the whipped tofu and lemon delight that she manufactured in great quantities and which, as Hugh said, transmuted the contents of one's stomach to liquid gold. Zach Singer, the oboe player came, and he played while ageless Frédérique Cyr danced, the humid air making a puddle of the mascara beneath her eyes. After supper, Gypsa McNider recited poetry in the clearing under the birches, her batwing sleeves arcing through the air as she declaimed that the amount of love in the world was constant. Her partner Tim lounged in the shadows rolling joints.

Hugh always sat well back in his chair, legs splayed, hands clasped over his stomach, arguing and drinking and drinking some more. He was a sculptor, and nature was his medium, for Hugh's art celebrated the transience of the day. He spoke of creating with the fundamental drive of a bee or a robin, but it was his personal mission to make manifest the passage of time. A spy out before dawn might glimpse Hugh crouched close to the earth, aligning the cedar fronds on the path to the dock, so that they all pointed like arrows at a newly sprung toadstool capped in neon tangerine. Days later, the fronds would be discovered placed in concentric circles honouring the fall of the same toadstool, its head now pockmarked and saggy with spores. Hugh alone knew how to rearrange a cob-web with a needle, scratch fern fronds onto a clear sheet of ice. The sight of Hugh lying face down on the dock, herding the skipping silver slips of the water beetles into a corral made of reeds threaded together on a horse hair filled Jan with the desire to shout out loud at the magnificence of life. His mode of being challenged Jan's conservative roots and attracted her, held her, and she would not, could not stop giving him her love, for his art, for his vision, for his great arms and fists and for the gold cap on his tooth.

"Stay," she said to him. "Stay always. My forest is your forest, my woods are your woods, my leaves your leaves, my lake your lake, my streams your streams." She could remember the silly loving burble of words even now.

Once Hugh made Jan a stained glass window, pieced together out of slips of mica leaded with reeds, glued with pine sap, girded with willow. The window was an impossible gift, and theirs was an impossible relationship, and yet it had lasted. For twenty years, the summer colony in the woods had been a place of refuge for artists of all kinds. Hugh did not know, but after a gust of wind shattered the mica window, Jan had searched the forest floor for shards. She kept them in an envelope under a floorboard in the bedroom.

In the beginning, Jan had considered Hugh's renunciation of permanence to be a grand and free gesture, like the operatic trilling of the hermit thrush or a soprano practising in a neighbouring house. She had honoured his anger when he had discovered her photographing his work. Hugh had knocked the camera out of her hand into the ferns, where she later picked it up, unharmed. *Get out,* he'd said. Get out of her own place. Extraordinary to think of it now, like that. And afterward he knelt before her and soaked her wraparound skirt with his tears.

"Your spirit is wide, Jan, like the horizon," he said, stretching out his arms to receive her. So she forgave him, and with him she felt forgiven.

Sometimes Jan found it unbearable that Hugh should have seen her aging. She ought to have drifted in and out of his life like one of his time-limited sculptures, here at dawn, gone in the evening, with the last trilling of the hermit thrush. Now she saw herself standing in the cold forest with an empty cardboard box in her thin hands. Her hair is shorter now, and she keeps it dark by artificial means, but she knows it disappoints people to come across her from behind, to have her turn to face them with the ridged pools of sleeplessness beneath her eyes.

Just as once upon a time Hugh found Jan, so he eventually found Crispin, one summer night in a bar on the Main in Montreal. Crispin was quick, wiry, and witty. In another century, he might have been a velvet-clad poet relishing his dreams, but Crispin was a water-colourist, producing exquisite works of the old school. They sold well. Dreamy clouds are never easy to achieve, but Crispin had a knack for painting the wide sky of Quebec on fire in the evening or nacreous at first light. Crispin's skies caught at the emotions, hinted at spiritual depths, but remained guileless, because when it came down to it, they were just sky, just water-colour.

Jan still has a photograph of Crispin at that time, lithe Crispin wearing a black halterneck with diamantes that stretch in a glittering curve into the hollows of his armpits. Earlier in the day, they had pulled up the chains and anchors on the dock and had paddled off on it as if it were a raft. Crispin swam around in the water, his wet head coppery in the sunlight. For a while, they had all wanted him.

Jan had tried hard. She maintained outward appearances with meals and money, but somewhere she lost the knack of renewing her love for Hugh each day and she found herself acting more as she felt she ought to, rather than from desire. The parties in the woods changed. Vernon Hasp's documentary about other men called Vernon Hasp attained cult status and he began to hold court in his own penthouse where he could see himself reflected in sixteen panes of glass at a time. Tiny drifted off to farm organic carrots. Frédérique died from complications following a hip replacement. Their places were taken by Crispin's friends: students, actors, musicians shouting at each other about Derrida and hip hop. Hugh was often absent from Jan's bed in the morning, but the woods revealed little trace of his work.

Jan knew better than to say anything. Hugh had every right to live as he wished. Early on, she did her crying on a city bus, during one of those winters when she taught photography at a community college. The tears erupted when she least expected it, pouring out with all the shame and inevitability of vomit onto the sidewalk, while the high-school kids sitting around her sank into their jackets and looked out the window.

The next summer, when they returned to the woods, Jan slept in the cabin and Hugh shuttled between her room and Crispin's in the Bunkie. One morning when she was out taking photographs, she came across Crispin perched on a rock, brooding in the steam that rose off the lake into the cool morning.

"I do love him, you know," he said.

"You know nothing of love," she replied. That morning, she took a photograph of a reed bending backwards into its sharply angled reflection. Around it quivered the lines of the water. The illusion of flexibility recalled her desire to share her streams and woods with Hugh, but when she looked at the bent reed, she also remembered how hard it was to share Hugh.

Later in the day, she woke Hugh from a nap, sat on the edge of the bed, spread out her hands on her knees, placed her ultimatum before him.

"I'm not cooking any more," she said.

"I never said you had to."

"I don't want you sleeping in the cabin any more."

"I'll leave if you want me to, Jan."

"No, you must stay, but stay in the Bunkie. I'm not leaving you." It was all she had left to say. She could forgive Hugh for Crispin. Perhaps Hugh had discovered some great and good love in himself with Crispin that he had never experienced with her. She even told herself that she could stop desiring Hugh, if that was what he wanted, but she could not stop caring.

They did not see a couples therapist, but they did see an architect; "the architect of our separation," she called the rotund little man in his office tower of reflecting glass. They renamed the main cabin the "Ruche" or hive, and constructed a network of simple buildings, half hidden in the bedrock or up on stilts, with shutters that hid the windows, and ferns that grew upon the roof. Fireplaces and rock ledges jutted out into the sitting rooms, and the buildings were joined by walkways with holes cut in them to accommodate the growth of the trees.

Jan built herself a studio where she worked on her photographs with an intensity that surprised her. Her subjects were clouds, trees, reflections. She made photo essays of the barns and shrines in the rural community around the lake, but she rarely took pictures of people. The only face for her remained Hugh's. He had a half-smile of such infinite sweetness, made the sweeter by his capacity to withhold it. She marked every day of their separation with a photograph: ice in the reeds, the coal-bright sparks on the lichen stalks, the water droplets that filled the lichen goblets to the brim.

And so the years had passed. During the summers, they lived in a scattered way among the trees, with Crispin, without Crispin, with Crispin again. And little by little Hugh's skin took on the transparency of age, and little by little, Jan's photographs became all the same. Up on the cliff top, with the empty container in her hand, Jan saw how she had lorded it over Hugh in her ownership of the paradise, and somewhere she had lost the natural line of herself, the line that swirled, was elastic and cut on the grain. Glorying in the idea of doing what she said she would do, she had given Hugh a place to stay, always, and in her stubbornness she had made chains for them both.

She had done what she said she would do. She had shared. By God, she shared everything that she had, and now when she finally had it all to herself, the wind lifting the roof in the old cabin, the rattle of flies against the glass in the studio, she found that she did not want it.

Perhaps Hugh had been right in his insistence that there should be nothing left to mark his passage in the world: no child, no artwork, no monument, nothing. Let the cabin and the studio on stilts fall into a careless teepee of boards in the forest, and beneath it a stained kapok mattress, its sodden insides spilling out into the leaf mould. Maybe there is no virtue, after all, in doing what you said you were going to do. Gone were the days of Frédérique lifting her chiffon scarves to the poplars. Jan shrugged. Now Hugh was gone too, and what was the point of holding on to anything? The time had come to pull her resentment out of herself, this anchor of hatred and love, and the gobbet of flesh that it was attached to. Up came the cable, dripping and straining, encrusted with zebra mussels and streaming weed. Mentally she flung it off the cliff after the ashes, left it to coil like a dead snake caught in a cedar tree.

Jan turned away from the cliff's edge and started back down the track. Out of habit she caught herself observing the funneled spider webs and the woodpecker holes, the flaps of lichen attached to the rock faces. It was November 20th, 2003 and Hugh had begun his passage into the ground, but she had no camera, no way to mark this day. Tomorrow the day would be gone. And now the tears came, for there was no other pair of eyes to see, to verify or to contradict her version of the vision. He was a bastard to have left her so alone.

Jan reached the bottom of the hill. In the distance, she could see the huddle of men beside the cars strung out along the road. Crispin was in the middle of the group, no longer young, but preserved by the passage of good scotch and regular exercise. Four young friends stood about, their beards groomed into neat pubic triangles. Hugh had been in thrall to them, more so than ever towards the end, trapped by loneliness and the camaraderie of rough young sex in tree houses.

The men looked at the cold sky and at the cold land, their hands thrust deep into their jacket pockets. Then they turned to look at her, expectant.

"Well, he's out there," she said, showing them the empty container. She waited for Crispin to speak. Now it was time to see what Crispin would make of the scattered remains of Hugh's love.

"God, I'm so very sorry," said Crispin, breathing in deeply and covering his face.

She stood looking at the backs of Crispin's hands, reddened and dry with cold, asparkle with short golden hairs. What was Crispin to her now? He was certainly not a son, or a brother, but some other relation—a step-partner, from whom she expected nothing, and to whom she owed nothing. And yet, she thought, it was true, she had also passed a life of sorts with Crispin.

Hugh was gone, but nothing was finished. Together they had built a colony, and the history of a colony is filled with coming, and going, and coming back again. The words came out of Jan before she could stop them.

"Stay," she said to Crispin. "Stay. Invite your friends. There's plenty of vegetable soup in the pot." Her mouth stretched sideways in an elastic line, and there was a give in it that she had forgotten.

Crispin took his hands away from his face and reached out to touch her forearm. His eyes appeared paler than ever now that he had taken to bleaching his hair.

"Thanks for the offer Jan," he said, "you've been a sweetie. But I think we'll head back into town. Mike has a gig tonight. Don't you Mike?"

A young man in black leather nodded, jingling his car keys.

"Right," said Jan. "Well. Come up whenever you feel like it." She turned away, holding herself rigid against the cold. Crispin stopped her as she was unlocking the car.

"Jan," he said, "Hugh stayed because he wanted to."

Jan spent the night at the cabin. She did not light the fire and she did not heat the soup. Instead she cocooned in the duvet and lay listening to the scuffle and twitter of mice in the walls. In the night the first snows came, and when she awoke she looked out at the fir trees and their green fingers, now outlined in white, spread wide and ready to bless. So that was it, she thought, the final benediction. She was forty-four, and free to go.

Salsa Madre

Photographs and translation by Jan McDonald

COME ON IN, don't be shy. My name is Bernadette. And you are? Jan. So pleased to meet you, Jan. Father René told me that you would stop by. Yes, I always work out here under the carport. I like the sound of rain falling on the roof. You're from Montreal? Toronto. Ah. That's a long way. I have a niece who lives there, on Yonge Street. Twins in a stroller, maybe you have seen her? They're a handful of trouble. Well, this is my summer project—should be finished in the next day or two. Sure, photos are fine. You might find the ground more stable for your tripod over on the path.

These are my tiles and pots and cups, arranged by colour. I do the actual smashing on the concrete, and I shape the pieces afterwards with nippers. I use an outdoors glue to fix the ceramic on the tub. Here's a nice piece of Limoges that Madame Benoit passed on to me. Look at the pink dress on that courtly lady, but see how it's cracked underneath? There's gold paint on it. I'll be using it somewhere special.

Today I prayed that the paint inside my shrine would stay put. I will not be ashamed to ask for that in the church, since my work is to glorify the Mother of Our Lord, so the paint should not flake no matter what I do. Not to say you shouldn't prime carefully. After all, our God is a busy God. I've seen shrines where the sun gets in and the paint hangs down in sheets around the head of the Holy Mother. She stands there as if she had her head up under a string of washing. Shame.

Mind you, not many people bother to keep up their shrines any more, and I don't know that you're going to find anything other than empty ones around here. These days people prefer deer on their lawns, or roosters or kids fishing. Down on Rue Bonaventure someone has an Olympic Stadium being attacked by a giant polar bear. Not many people feel that much faith any more, or if they do, they keep it in their pockets and not in their gardens, except at Christmas, and then it's the plastic figurines. Violette La Caisse bought an entire set on sale at the hardware store and they faded after two years. You can't make holy things out of plastic.

I've been doing ceramic stars on my bathtub, rays or petals of one colour and centres of another. I stick them on first, and then I fill in the gaps with little bits left over. Mother Mary approves of recycling. She gave birth in a barn, after all, even though where she is now she probably has most things in gold and jasper. I gave her a good clean this morning. She looks nice lying on the grass, doesn't She? Resting. Just like my mother used to have a little siesta after lunch.

I expect Father René told you that I was once a novice. I was about to take my vows when God came to me in a dream. He said go to the general store, so I did. I was so shy! The store was nothing like the supermarkets we have now. You could get anything there. Violette La Caisse was the cashier that day.

Urgel Beauregard from up Lac des Tortues way came in. I didn't know him from Adam, but I heard him say to Violette that his wife had died and would she have him, because he had six children and didn't know what he would do. And Violette said thanks for offering, but she had enough on her hands with the rush on sugar pie orders, and she turned to serve me and I looked up at Urgel's big empty eyes. He drove a truck for the paper mill, and I brought up all those children in this house and we had two more of our own. Good kids. They all pitched in.

Now I'm going to tell you what happened to my son Henri. It's nothing you won't hear from down the road. Still, I'd rather tell you in my own words. People say that divorce is the worst thing that can happen to a family, but there are worse things. It's the same with families as it is with ceramic. You don't quite know how the tile will crack, even if you think you have a rough idea. I'm talking hairline cracks, places where it's ready to break and we can't tell until the hammer comes down. Well, whatever went on used to happen in the vestry. And in the end my boy Henri got so quiet I knew something was up. He was not the only one. And next thing they sent that priest to the South of France so that he could do it all over again in the sun.

When Henri turned sixteen, he went to work in his uncle's fish shop in Montreal. Plenty of boys do it. I suppose they think there's more to life down there. Hard to imagine, isn't it? When we have all this sky up here. But at least he told me he was going—he could have gone to do squeegee like that kid down the road. I left him alone. You have to let people work things out, but I never stopped wondering how he was, and I never stopped praying for him. He was a good kid.

You know, about this time last year the Virgin Mary appeared to me behind the barn. I was spraying the lettuces with a slug killer that I make by boiling up cigarette butts. It works a charm. Well, all of a sudden I had this feeling that there was a mystery happening beyond the edge of the vegetable patch. And I came around the corner of the barn, and there She was, hovering over the lightning weed. Just small, like a figurine, but shimmering. And she said to me in a voice as low as a mourning dove's, *Find what was lost, renew what has been broken, give the thanks that is due.* I fell down to my knees and I cried and I cried.

Well, what can you do when the Holy Mother calls? I went to Montreal on the bus and stayed with my cousin's friend Rosalia. She lives near the Jean Talon market. So beautiful this market, with the fruit laid out in the shops—pink carrots, pink! There are organic bananas spooning to the left, aubergines spooning to the right, and prickly fruits from Asian countries that I don't even know the name of. I bought a lot of tomatoes for only five dollars, and Rosalia and I spent all afternoon making a sauce called salsa madre, which is very good and has more garlic in it than Urgel would ever let me use at home. I had no problem discovering where Henri was living. He has an apartment in the Church of Our Lady of the Immaculate Conception, only now it's condos. Early in the morning I sat in the band rotunda in the park, and I saw them come out of the door, my Henri, and a little boy, and another man.

The boy sat on Henri's shoulders and held onto his ears for balance. Henri's friend held the door open for them, shut it carefully behind them. The urge to get up and run to them, God help me, it was so strong. My feet were rising off the ground, but I held onto the railings with both hands. I watched them walk all the way down the street to the car, a nice car. Then I went back to Rosalia's and got the jars of salsa madre, and then I returned to the church that is now condos. A young man with a ponytail let me into the building. He had a T-shirt on that said "Don't shut me in." I looked at him and said with my eyes, "Don't shut me out," and he opened the door, just like that.

Inside, you can't imagine what they have done to the Church of Our Lady. They have built a hotel in there, and left one pew to sit on while you wait for the elevator. Where there should be a stoup, just inside the door, there is a water cooler. And where the Cardinal walked on marble flagstones in 1961, there is carpet and a corridor. Well I've done the same thing in the other direction, me out here turning my bathtub into a sacred place. We're all going in one direction or another, and who's to say it won't become a church again in a hundred years? Likewise, if you needed a bathtub, you could come and dig up one of those empty shrines from down the road.

From Henri's apartment on the fifth floor you can see the whole city. A young woman was there, doing the cleaning. Such a tiny girl from some Asian country. She could see I was his mother, and she showed me right in. Oh, you have never seen such an apartment! So tidy, so calm, like a monastery, with slanted windows high in the ceiling, and a shining aluminum refrigerator, and a bedroom up a spiral staircase. I delivered my jars of salsa madre, and the girl stood on a chair and put them in an empty cupboard high up, and we lined up the jars just so and closed the doors. Henri will find them on a hungry day, a day when he cannot think what to cook, and he can use that sauce with the vegetables that he might already have.

So that was it. I came home. I don't like Montreal. Too much concrete. But at least I know that he is living in the house and heart of Our Lady, and he is safe. And I am glad, and grateful for Prayers Answered. And so I wait, in case Henri wants to bring that child home to meet his grandmother, because that is the next thing that I will pray for, as I pray for the man who held the door open, and the mother of the child, too, whoever she is. I will wait and watch for Henri to come in his own time, same as I wait for the deer to come out of the forest to eat the new shoots on the field. And then, what a feast we will have.

Look, Jan—I am ready for the *coulis*. What is the word for *coulis* in English? Yes, grout. The colour of this grout is called paprika, which will spice up all that blue and make the yellow bright in the rain. So we mix up the *coulis* with water, until it's thick and sloppy like icing, and then we work it on with a spatula, like this, into the cracks, and then scraping off the excess, and then doing it again. Here we go. And now we give a good polish with our cloth, *et voilà*, the colours come together and my bath becomes a shrine fit for Our Lady of Lowing Cows, Our Lady of Meltwater, Our Lady of Lightning Weed, Our Lady of Blackened Shingles, Our Lady of the Smelter, Our Lady of Everywhere.

Without the *coulis,* the broken cups and saucers are just that, broken. And without the ceramic, the *coulis* is just wet earth. But put both together, and they glow. The *coulis* is love. We cannot do without it. You have kids, Jan? Just your books of photographs? Well, it's all for the glory. Will you listen to that blackbird? He's up there every evening. Let me wash my hands and I'll make you some coffee. You won't find a better cup down the road.

Champlain's Astrolabe

FUELLED BY A COFFEE of mythic proportions, Brian Armstrong drove eastwards from Toronto in a mood so foul it made his flesh cold and his armpits sweat. Brian hated site visits in Quebec. Why couldn't Irwin have sent him to photograph the Bahamas project instead? Beyond Montreal there must have been a hundred groundhogs perched on their burrows in the weak spring sunshine or squashed along the sandy shoulders of the road. Brian would have liked to wrap up a few of the riper ones and courier them back to Irwin as a present. Still, in the car he at least felt safe from the hovering clouds of French vowels that swirled in the air outside. The deeper he got into the province, the more roly-poly the French accent would become and the less likely it was that he would ever understand a word of it. Men, women and children: a whole province-full of people talking through a mouthful of steel wool. The main thing was not to stop until he got to the site at Lac Yahoo.

Irwin had assured Brian that the client was an English-speaking photographer from Ontario with a vacation home in Quebec. She wanted an organic look for her new buildings, so there would be trees to save, which he knew Brian would appreciate. Brian cared less for the trees than Irwin realized. Brian was hoping for a small-waisted, red-maned, green-eyed, fearless photographer. And not just a photographer, but a pilot too, or better still, a trapeze artist. Evidently she was a friend of Vernon Hasp, the film director. Not that Brian ever got invited to those parties. He never went anywhere. Not strictly true. Shortly after the divorce he had visited a resort where he had eaten a bad mussel. He had returned to find his electricity bills strangely elevated because Kelvin had installed a small grow op in the basement.

Kelvin had always been a question-mark kid. Whenever Brian thought about what to do with him, his mind developed black and white static like an old television. The boy might be awake by now, lounging in his chair in the half-light, prisms reflected off the computer screen jiggling their way across the lenses of his glasses. Kelvin was all caught up in some kind of game. He said he had hoards of imaginary charm, plenty of character and wealth stored in the basement computer. Kelvin had lately turned twenty-one but the basement still smelt of socks and apple cores.

Spring rain began to fall and Brian turned on the wind-shield wipers, found a Vermont radio station and got into the rhythm of the road. He noted a host of white birds feeding in a drowned field beside the river and even found himself able to appreciate the rumpled heads of the nut-brown pampas grass and the barrow-shaped clumps of sumac. Every stalk and bole was tinged with the green-gold of spring sap rising. And as for the billboards advertising local bars, each was a teenager's dream, dominated by a pair of bronzed goddesses coiled around poles, fully trained in the slithery arts of Bourbon Street and just waiting to entertain the weary trucker or the lonely man from the architectural firm in his crappy car.

For a few kilometres Brian returned to one of his favourite fantasies: a willing woman in a dry sugar shack with a clean floor and no cobwebs. What such a woman would be doing in a sugar shack this late in the season Brian was not sure, but it did not matter. The stickiness and the sweetness were all.

After the rain stopped the margins of the sky lay fringed and ragged with mist along the tops of the birch forest. By his calculations, Brian was not far off from the artists' colony at Lac Whoozie, but the mega-coffee weighed heavily in his bladder. He pulled off onto a side road for four-wheelers. No need to risk going into a café. A quick whiz in the woods and he could be back on the road. He tucked his wallet out of sight, pressed the button to lock the door and shut it firmly. It would be a disaster if the camera were stolen.

A ditch full of pampas grass and a low wire fence lay between him and the woods. He made an awkward leap and got across with only one boot soaked. He stepped over the fence, ducked in behind the trees and stood looking up through the branches as if he had never met himself, while he listened to the stream and sputter on the damp layers of foliage at his feet.

Afterwards, Brian walked on into the woods a few paces in order to stretch his legs. He kept his eyes on the ground in case there was treasure to be discovered. Leaves of dogtooth violet slanted in fat green stitches across the leaf mould. Brian had always envied the retired electricians of Great Britain, swinging their metal detectors over the sodden furrows, drawn to the unmistakable edge of metal rising out of the dull clods. Nose guards, helmets, pommels, cinctures: the biting beast and its winking garnet eye; words that spoke of gold warmed by a good grip had always excited him.

He stopped before a pool of snow water. An object lay at the bottom of it. It was a metal disk, dull and serrated: a winch, a gear, cog-like. It could have been Champlain's Astrolabe, only that had already been found.

Astrolabe sounded like one of the drugs that Cynthia had been prescribed for depression. Cynthia's psychotherapist had been as dedicated to ending Brian's marriage as any divorce lawyer. As it turned out, Brian was the one with the problem, and Cynthia just needed a boyfriend.

After she got herself into therapy, but before she reduced Brian to driving a car without cupholders, Cynthia had discovered that Brian was the reason why their son Kelvin had buried himself in the basement, draping his shoulders with the pixilated garments of the medieval role player. With the blessing of her therapist, Cynthia had called Brian immature: until he took control of his own life he could not be a proper father for Kelvin, or, by happy coincidence, a proper partner for Cynthia. Brian had never met Cynthia's therapist. He had a thing or two he would like to say to her.

Brian prodded at the metal disk with his foot. It was junk. Champlain's Astrolabe, now that had been a true treasure.

Brian would have liked to have been the boy who found it, but at least he had not been the man who dropped it. Poor Champlain, vertiginous with anxiety as the pole star came up and he found himself in a land whose known reach extended no further than the length of his bug-bitten arms. The feeling of visceral dropping away would be as bad as misplacing your keys in the forest, or locking them inside the – and here Brian had a moment of clarity – locking them inside the car in the middle of Quebec.

Brian stood very still, trying to think what to do. He looked around him, as if the very trees were about to start making incomprehensible sounds.

What did Champlain do after he lost his astrolabe? He walked on into the unknown. Brian walked on. He came to the edge of a cleared field and saw ahead of him a tumulus-shaped hill topped by a Quonset hut, its front end ringed in lights. A large billboard dominated the corner of the field. *Danseuses 7 Jours*. Brian's French was improving.

He set out across the field towards the building, his boots sinking into the ridges between the cold stubble of last year's corn stalks. Clods of earth attached themselves to the soles of his boots until he felt weighed down like a giant. With a bit of luck *Danseuses 7 Jours* might also mean women dancing at eleven o'clock in the morning.

He crossed the gravel parking lot, pushed open the metal door under the lights and ducked as a sparrow came flying out. He wondered what other problems the building had apart from animal infestation. A cleverly curved wall of mirrors ran

37

down one side. In front of the mirrors were a couple of empty risers and three vacant aluminum poles. The bar was at the far end of the room, beyond the high tables and a jukebox that glowed in a rainbow of light. Brian peered into the dim distance where a dash of red moved rhythmically near the bar. Could it be the glimmer of light on a ruby tassel? *How little I really know about Quebec,* he thought. *Gallic societies are so much more generous than Anglo-Saxon ones, when it comes to tassels.*

No tassels. Just a woman wearing the longest red and black plaid overshirt that Brian had ever seen. She was mopping the floor with sullen strokes. Her eyebrows met head to head like embattled tadpoles, squaring off at each other whenever she frowned over the tanned arrow of her nose. Her ears and nostrils glimmered with pierced gold. Every so often she stopped and sucked in her cheeks, as if life had given her a drink with a disagreeable taste, to be taken through a straw at regular intervals.

Brian took his boots off to show his goodwill towards the woman with the mop. He put his hands up in a gesture of submission while he walked in slowly, saying "anglaisie anglaisie." All he wanted was a drink and a chance to use the phone, although the thought occurred to him that mopping might be part of her routine.

She must have read his thoughts, for she pulled him half a pitcher of Rickard's, poured the first glass and brought it over to the table. Brian was glad for such generous, speechless understanding. Under the plaid thing she must surely be narrow-waisted, full-breasted. What did Champlain do when he met strange women? He addressed them cheerfully.

"Here's to the heroes," said Brian, waving his glass at a newly framed photograph of Les Canadiens holding aloft the Stanley Cup. The woman turned away unsmiling and began spraying the counter out of a squeeze bottle.

Brian watched her, entranced. Perhaps the problem with Kelvin was that he had yet to find a girlfriend. What he needed was a woman whose touch shocked him, whose presence confused his thought processes, who rendered his entire body as brilliantly lit as a landing strip. Brian had felt that way about Cynthia, at the beginning. Once he had narrowly escaped a collision between his bike and a car. At the time he had been thinking about the way Cynthia's eyelashes cast shadows on her cheeks.

Maybe a brush with mortality was what Kelvin needed. Not the serious kind of brush that would leave you armless or tin-faced or worse, but the positive kind of cathartic full-length body shiver that made you relieved to be alive; eager to find out what was next. Initiation. Was that what it was about? Scarification rituals, raiding parties, controlled bloodletting and long walkabouts in cracked dry lands. Surely every culture had a way of galvanizing teenaged slothfulness into energetic adulthood? Brian had only to think of the Canadian way. He considered himself to have had his own brush with mortality at eighteen, when he'd worked a summer for his grandfather, a lumber-camp foreman in the age of the mechanized saw. Arguing and chain-smoking they had driven for hours into northern Ontario until the cratered bush road finally brought them to a settlement of Quonset huts in a clearing. There a tribe of rank sweaty bears with chainsaws drove themselves day and night in the single-minded testosterone-fuelled ecstasy of a back-country lumber camp in full swing.

A blaze had broken out in an adjacent sector and Brian remembered his entire body shaking as he stood mesmerized by the sight of crown fire leaping from tree to tree across the crest of the hill, roaring like a locomotive on the move. They had made a run for it in the truck, and days later Cynthia, still in her gin-fizz waitressing days, had wrapped her long arms around him when she heard the story, and had murmured something into the still smoky shirt (he had not washed it) and he had said, *what?* She had repeated the words, and he still had not understood, but he had pretended to. That had been the beginning of their relationship.

Yes, a good galvanizing brush with death, that was what Kelvin needed. Not role-playing HriÞkringle the Bard of the Basement; not altercations with the pizza delivery man. But wait, hadn't there been a school friend of Kelvin's who had been sent home in a box from one of those places where you are thirsty all day? Now that Brian thought about it, that kind of thing could throw you off balance. Somalia or the Sudan? Cynthia would know. It was a pity that they were not talking.

Obviously the woman behind the bar was not going to do anything but clean. Brian downed the last of the beer and, as he felt for his wallet, recalled tucking it under the floor mat of the car.

He looked at the mopping woman, raising his open hands in a multilingual apologetic and exasperated shrug. Then he opened up his jacket and pointed at the empty space where the wallet ought to be. Surely she would understand that. He was just bringing his hand up into the gesture of an imaginary telephone and was considering how to mime that he would be back to pay after the automobile association had unlocked the car, when a man built like a fire hydrant emerged from the shadows, head butted him off his stool, shoved him back towards the door, grabbed him by the arm and tossed him out into the parking lot.

Life flashing before your eyes and all that: there's not as much time as you might think when you are being flung through the air. In Brian's case all he experienced was a brief sensation of passing through a cool column of air followed by the impression that the gravel reached up and pulled him down, blasting its sharp points into his shoulder. All he managed to think was: *and now my head goes down,* which it did, hard.

For some minutes Brian found himself unwilling to leave the horizontal world where the vertical mottled stripe of the parking lot softened into bulging green hillocks and where the rain apparently fell upwards like bubbles in an aquarium. Meanwhile the last battle of the cosmos had come upon him. Giants were uprooting burning trees out of his left temple and tossing them into a frazzled prism that had appeared in his right eye.

He flinched and rolled as his boot struck him in the chest. He grabbed it, and rolled over to avoid the other boot, which did not follow. Finally he sat up, rubbing his shoulder and the side of his face. It felt as if his arm had been wrenched out of its socket.

What had Brian been thinking about? That Kelvin needed a brush with death. Maybe so.

"But not my death," he said in a low croak, breaking into a hunch-backed run, feeling strangely exhilarated by the lacerating bite of the gravel through the thinning soles of his socks.

All the Voices Cry

I HATE TO ADMIT IT, but I missed the turnoff. So many trees came down in last summer's storm that I may have mistaken the markers. The landscape looks different when it's all humps and mounds and puffed out sails of snow. A person lost in the woods walks in a curve, so perhaps I will return to the cabin, eventually.

Otto would never have cut back in a loop through the woods. He would have persevered in a straight line across the lake, headlong into the howling wind, even if he'd had to crawl, frosted to the ear tips. *Freya, Freya, don't be a darlink idiot.* Czech gave his English a glinting edge that could cut my polite Canadian vowels to shreds in an argument.

It has been eight years now since Otto's death and I often catch myself acting without consulting him. The first mechanical movements are long past, when I begrudged my own body's instinct to continue breathing. Indoor plants have come and gone. I have bought a bicycle. All the life-sustaining illusions about the importance of winter hats and true love have begun to reassert themselves. But after thirty years together it is not surprising that I should still be prone to phantom conversations. The mind twitches, remembering.

It is a difficult thing, to know when one is ready to lay aside the cloak of widow's weeds, and to seek a new mate, a lover, or perhaps to begin with, someone to stand beside at parties. This idea of setting out to find someone new, for example. Otto would have considered it predatory, the kind of thing the witchy Baba Yaga side of me would do. Whenever Baba Yaga made an appearance—usually when I got angry about the spread of zebra mussels and the wicked passage of purple loosestrife through the waterways—Otto would disappear outside to the woodpile, take up his axe and chop, leaving Baba Yaga to fume and clank about in the kitchen.

These days, Baba Yaga is feeling quite proactive. She has wheel-clamped the chicken foot that holds up her house. She does not want potential suitors to be nauseated by intemperate spinning. In the evenings she stands before the mirror speaking nicely to the imaginary princes who have arrived at her door clutching bouquets of blue roses. *Oh but how lovely. Let me just get a vase.* She notices a fragment of squirrel flesh caught in her tooth, hurries off to find a toothpick.

Oh, but I have accepted that Otto is not here. Like Baba Yaga's princes, he is also imaginary, even though I can see him walking beside me in his heavy plaid coat. How many times did I sew the buttons back onto that coat? Baba Yaga and I have a right to regenerate our lopped off limbs. Yes we do.

This walking is such work. My snowshoes are failing me. Each step is a voyage downwards into the icy shadows that swallow me up to mid-thigh. Pushing against the sucking softness, I heft my foot out and make a tiny moonstep before falling headlong into the drift. When I stop I hear my heart beating and the plump sound of snow pushed out of the trees by passing gusts of wind. There is snow in my eyelashes and up my sleeves. Sweat makes its way between my breasts in silver runnels. This is as juicy, as marinated, and as edible as I get.

What if a curious accident were to befall me? What if a bear, awake with spring hunger pains, should shamble out of the woods? There is a book about a woman who takes a bear for a lover, isn't there? Baba Yaga could take the bear home to dine on blueberry cobbler and salmon pie. Better that than a quick clobber and the hot fang of death.

Is a bear in the bed better than two lovers separated by death? I don't know, but I would not mind finding out. The next time I find myself seated at the library computer terminals beside the man in Red Suspenders, I will ask him out for coffee. And I will smile a lot, for despite the glitter of platinum in my back teeth, the smile on the outside is still good. And no matter what Red Suspenders does, no matter if he tells me about online tax calculations or compares long distance phone plans, Baba Yaga will say, *why yes, do tell me more.*

A deer has just come out of the woods. Dainty best describes the pattern of spots on her sides, like icing sugar on a coffee cake, and the tender white flame of a tail. *Let nature lead you, Freya.* My father used to say that. He was a wise man, a woodsman, and well read. He kept a notebook filled with his favourite Norse sayings, like *the forest is the best teacher for a boy.* So, following Papa's advice, and ignoring Otto's, I will follow the deer's tracks. She has been running high on the banks beside the road where the purple brusilla grows in the summertime, and I have been struggling along in the ruts. But now I know where I am. I have arrived at the artists' colony.

They were quite the pair, those artists. They used to drive across from Toronto for the summer, arriving in Quebec with all the excitement and release of being in a different country. He built sculptures throughout the woods at all hours of day and night, and she was a photographer, drooping about with her hair in her eyes. He was stocky and she was willowy. Otto called them the Rock and the Reed. We used to take visitors to the outskirts of the artists' terrain to see the Rock's work. It was worth the walk to see the faces carved into the clay banks of the stream, or the huge mobiles made of leaves and horse-hair. Some visitors murmured about scribbles on water when they saw the sculptor's work, others said he must be a maniac. Once, when Otto and I took my father on this walk, the Rock saw us photographing a pile of leaves arranged in a spiral. He rushed towards us, shouting, not unlike a short polar bear with his shaggy chest and bristling white head.

"The Rock is drunk," Otto said, turning away. My father, on the other hand, tapped his pipe out on a tree and refilled it, saying, *"Speak of trolls and they rustle in the hallway."*

Sheltered by the low eaves, there is less snow up here on the boardwalk that joins the assorted cabins and studios together. There's a banging sound coming from the summer kitchen. Perhaps it's squatters. The artists won't mind squatters. They share everything. I can see from here that the storm door has been wedged open by a drift. I might be offered a hot drink.

We might have a talk about my Baba Yaga problems. Squatters know a lot about society, being in it and out of it at the same time. This is snooping, Freya, it will gain you nothing, peering in at the empty easel, the jar of cobwebbed brushes: *At every doorway, ere one enters, one should spy round.*

I'll just trot along and have a look.

Many summers ago a new dog took off on us, spooked by the unfamiliar give and snap of the forest floor. Otto and I wandered the woods all afternoon whistling and calling. Eventually we arrived here at the colony. We heard raised voices inside the summer kitchen, and the heavy groan of female exasperation. And then the avocado shot out the door, powering into the sunlit grove.

How richly endowed with feeling, how proper it seemed to me at that moment, to hurl avocados in times of passion and of rage. The sunlight descended through the canopy of trees in blue yellow shafts, illuminating the bright thistledown of the Rock's hair where he stood blocking the doorway. She meant to get him, the throw was hard, but passion warped the trajectory. Sailing past the sculptor's ear out the screen door the green missile landed on the rock in front of us, its froggy innards slipping out from beneath the tough skin pushed awry.

At that time there was no electricity and no road access to the cabins on the lake. Otto and I were still bringing our food across by canoe. The waste of the avocado suddenly appalled us both. We crept away in silence.

Today I would not say no to rage, or to any other kind of feeling.

What is this banging in the kitchen? A can has just thudded out through the screen door, tumbling low and making heavy progress. Looks like some one has been trying to open it with a screwdriver. Tossed aside, smeared with ketchup and flour, the side dented, the label slashed with what look like— claws. Ye gods and mortals. *Speak of trolls and they rustle in the hallway.*

Any minute now that bear will sense me with his flour-frosted snout, hunger and frustration all he knows. Now I cannot hear anything except for our breathing, the bear's and mine. Baba Yaga and Red Suspenders and passion be damned. A bear is not a sustaining illusion. A bear is.

Oh my. Where have I got to in all this?

Shuffle back shuffle back, clatter off the walkway while the crows lift off the treetops and all the voices cry, *Freya, Freya, we walk in the woods alone my dear, walk in the woods alone.*

To Catch a Fish

POOR MAURICE. He failed, but until I walked in the door at the cabin neither of us knew that it was a test, to catch a fish. How much easier for both of us if I had presented him with a room of straw to spin into gold, or had asked him to grow a peony, with a sunrise in its midst and the clouds of morning gathered in its petals.

Here is how it happened. I had been walking into the deepening dusk for an hour, just a grey-haired woman with a backpack and a stick. Not that a stick is much use against the ranging horsefly. Still, I don't mind flies. They are alive, and so am I. We are two species sharing the same pink evening air, the short green fields and the rectangular lumps of vanilla fudge that resolve into cows when I put my glasses on. I told Maurice not to come and get me. For the first time, he had his own guests at my cabin that night – Stewart Blaney, the antique dealer and his new wife Noreen. I was happy that he was making himself at home.

Here's how Maurice's voice sounds, booming out into the twilight, causing the birds to twitter with anxiety and the fish to stir in the waters.

Oh ho, Stewart, Noreen, glad you found us. Bienvenus au Lac Perdu. Were my directions adequate? It's the real boondocks out here. Come on in. Bathroom, second tree on your left past the screened porch. Don't look so worried Noreen. Come and sit down, Stewart. Isn't this view tremendous? There you are Noreen. Wine for the lady. Yes, Freya will be in soon. She's en route from Quebec. New granddaughter. Over-protective grandma. You know the story.

My granddaughter Tessie is six weeks old and already sorting out the difference between day and night, clever little thing. Her fists curl up like fiddleheads. Mia is marvellous, rushing about with diapers and laundry, laying Tessie down like a fish in the scale, crowing over her daily weight gains.

What's that Stewart? How long? Six weeks alone in the bee-loud glade. Yes, bloody loud, exactly. Bored? Me? Not at all. Swim each morning, a walk, books. I've been digging compost into a peony bed for Freya. My word, the Giant Hogweed is the stuff of nightmares. Strikes you blind you know.

I think I'll pick a few wildflowers for the table. They won't be up to Maurice's standard—hawkweed and viper's bugloss are hardly offerings to bring a peony grower. Maurice with his strains and names. To tell the truth, peonies have never appealed to me. Showy at first, they soon become so shaggy and overblown. I prefer my weeds with their shy flowers and tenacious root systems.

No, retirement suits me just fine, but don't get me wrong, the goddess of Real Estate was good to me. I have ridden the waves, so to speak, always holding onto the basic notion of what makes a good investment, and I was prepared to put the work in, just as Freya and Otto did here. The value of this property has increased, not just because of their input, but because the city has grown closer. I believe that Otto carved the newel posts. Very good with his hands. Learned his craft in Eastern Europe.

Maurice is intuitive about cultural things, and he's a talker, which is marvellous after Otto's silence, which became heavier as he got older. Wine, flowers, the best recording of a Strauss opera; Maurice always knows. I'll be on the point of feeling under-informed when he'll say something about the dense blue of the woods across the lake, or snort at the explosion of a four-wheeler on the road, and I know that he understands. We come at the same thing but from different angles.

No, there are no motorboats on this lake, which is a pity. Hard to get the wind in your hair in an antique birchbark canoe. I've been meaning to ask Freya if we can change the rules. It's all done by communal agreement. No, of course you wouldn't want the locals with their Sea-Doos, but there's nothing wrong with the chug of a vintage motor. Didn't bother the fish back in the twenties, so I don't see why it would now. Freya's a bit of a purist in that regard. I believe they only put the electricity through here about ten years ago. Amazing isn't it, what you can do by lamplight? Now then Stewart, none of that.

Maurice has walked this country road to the post office and back several times since I have been away. I can see him thwacking at the heads of yarrow with his stick, whistling to the blackbirds, imitating, fitting in, as he does. I wonder if he burps back at the frogs. There is an old-fashioned courtliness about Maurice's onion-skin writing paper that lures me back to him, like breadcrumbs tossed out for birds.

My dear Freya,

Before dawn I donned the bug suit, raked the poor earth beside the driveway to a fine tilth and went about flinging poppy seeds like a figure in a French painting. Three blue jays shrieked their advice from the hemlock. A positive tempest yesterday. Hurricanoes and waterspouts raging over the lake and thunder fit to crack the heavens. Come to me soon, and see the bed that I have prepared for you.

Until then, my darling F., from your darling M.

Grief dulls the edges of life. But love, like rain, washes the morning fresh and makes the next day possible. I have been so relieved to feel my spirit quickening at the thought of Maurice; to marvel again at the smooth decline on a man's thigh just below the hip bone, to discover tenderness stealing in even as I visit the supermarket and observe the pale white rootlets at the end of a bunch of chives. Otto was my husband, but Maurice is my lover. Maurice is teasing and skilled, which means that I stride towards him in the night and that I am surprised and greatly pleased by what we make possible together. The sweet stress of pleasure makes me feel green and hardy. I can smell the lilac on the evening air.

And now, my friends, you are going to fish for your supper. I believe that the local poissons are ready to leap onto our hooks in the best bucolic style. Lake's teeming with them. Come on down to the dock. Don't forget your hat Noreen, wonderful hat.

Otto and I put the dock in the water in 1973, the year that Mia was born. Each summer I sit down there in my Adirondack chair watching the fish hover over their nests in the beer-brown shallows. The parental gesture is protective, gentle and enduring. I have seen generations of fish come and go. Matriarch of fish: fish-mother, that's me. Last July I spent hours brooding over the fish fanning their tails above the silt and all the while I thought of baby Tess developing in the womb. How I wished her well in every sinew and soft bone.

First blood to the lady Noreen. Marvellous. Bit small, but there's nothing like a tasty mouthful. Hup. And another. Refill Stewart? My mother used to talk about days like this with the Laurentian Club. Lac Edouard was a positive turmoil of trout. Local guides, tea boiling in a real Australian billy. No, these fish are Perchaudes. A bass with a big or a small mouth. Can't remember which. Does yours have a large mouth, Noreen? Marvellous quality of stillness here in the evening. The recipe calls for a pound of fillets, but these little chaps should do us nicely. And now, my friends, to the kitchen.

Otto and I courted on the back of a motorbike in the streets of Prague, but I insisted that we make our home in Canada. *Qui prend mari prend pays,* they say in Quebec, but in our case it was *qui prend femme prend famille,* and I had a large one that I could not leave. We built the cabin together, replanting maples, tending to the moss, hiding the roof in a turf cloak spotted with hawkweed stars in the spring. When I saw the joy that Otto took in holding Mia when she was a baby, I thought that I had done the right thing, bringing him to Quebec, taking him out of his element.

*Let me just get this avocado going here, and the garlic, like so.
I get wonderful garlic up at the market. Rosy as a breast each clove
– they bring it in from Provence. There's a village there and garlic
is all that they do. The village down the road does breath mints. Oh
that blessed Oka cheese. Now you my lovely Noreen, may take your
knife to the chives.*

I entered just as the meal was being served. The lamp on
the table illuminated simple platters of baked potatoes, unc-
tuous with melted cheese, fresh greens, a sprinkle of herbs.
Upon a red enamel serving dish, the tiny bodies of the mother
fish lay in a fragrant heap, dusted in flour and spices, cooked
quickly in fresh butter and drizzled with a lemon and lime
sauce. I kissed everyone on both cheeks, smiled, took my por-
tion, and left it on the side of my plate. The meal progressed,
the wine travelled round and round, and finally, finally, the
Blaneys left.

"Great people, the Blaneys. What it is to have friends, eh
Freya?"

"Maurice, those people are not my friends. You just ate
my friends."

We failed each other. I could not make Maurice see how
the work of thirty years could be thus betrayed in a skillet, and
as for Maurice, well, his response was to call me a dear, silly
old thing, which only transformed me into a nasty beast with
prickles.

After that things went as you might expect: a silent bed
with two far-flung continents in it, the inevitable return to
town, and my return to the cabin, alone. Maurice must have

crouched on the shore with his knife, scraping the fish as the dusk deepened around him. All summer long, translucent scales have worked their way out of the sandy beach, curved like a baby's fingernail, but fluted at the edge.

The Tenured Heart

FROM BEHIND THE wheel of the inert Volvo, Associate Professor Colin Pilchard conceded that up in the woods, life, no longer simple, develops myriad complications. Accustomed to the striped shade of the university library, the academic body (pallid, unattached, in need of a haircut) becomes wreathed in rashes of unidentifiable origin. The academic mind, calibrated to accommodate issues and theories, finds itself at a loss to construe the rapid passage of the ground shrew, the wisp-thin lines of the spider's web or the irrational oscillations of the poplar leaf. The tenured heart, usually preserved in the dim formaldehyde of ethical behaviour, tends towards unconstrained lurches.

The women down on the dock could be considered a case in point. About now they would be raising their eyebrows at the silence that followed the strained twirling sound of a motor lacking the juice to start. Apparently, one of them had left the headlights on and car doors wide open, with the express purpose of letting the battery run down. Colin leaned back and let out a broken adolescent yowl at a rip in the vinyl ceiling of the car. The culprit would be towelling her hair dry, her backbone still sparkling with water drops. Her name was Sam and she was a perfect naiad; she could have been born wearing the pale blue bikini.

July had already been in bloom a few weeks when Colin had received the invitation to visit the cottage at Lac Perdu. The lake below the university rose up in a cloud and hovered among the trees, the sun winked off the windshields in the parking lot, but the concrete corridors of the English department remained as still and dry as an ancient seabed. In the dim light of his office, Professor Pilchard idled in his computer chair. He was halfway through an email.

…wondering if you would be interested to join us for a week-end at our cottage on the shores of Lac Perdu? I know that it is far from town, practically in another country, but the water feels like velvet at this time of year.

Some three years earlier, in the course of her Master's degree, Samantha de la Tour had attended closely to Professor Pilchard's group discussions of writers who regularly lost all their friends and relations in labyrinthine libraries, who made mosaics out of dull fragments joined with pale grey effusions of guilt, who repeated themselves until the meaning rose like spume over surf, evanescent and impossible to recapture from one day to the next. Colin Pilchard made it his business to listen to his students as if they were instruments in an orchestra and he conducted his tutorials accordingly, setting the bright and the dull voices against each other, adding new ideas to further the development, and using his invisible baton to direct the chorus towards a falling cadence of mutual consent.

Occasionally he pre-recorded his opinions, so that he could sit back and argue with himself in the third person, employing the same discernment as his students.

Among these students, Samantha de la Tour stood out for her refusal to accept any interpretation without question. Sam, who could pour her attention onto a text like a thread of clear water that magnified as it ran. Sam, who had flashed into the department for two years, perched on window seats, and darted out again, like a cardinal on the wing. Graduate students: now you see them, now they are gone, gone. But where? to teach Japanese people to speak English, to work in advertising, to survive for three months as poets, to retrain as lawyers.

I hope you won't think this invitation inappropriate, but since my MA at Rook U is long since finished... Let me know, and I can send you directions.

Kind regards

Sam de la Tour

Consider it Sam? He had dreamed of it.

As he drove northeast towards Sam's cottage in Quebec, Colin Pilchard contemplated a conference abstract about the monosyllable as *the thing itself,* because the monosyllable says what it means to say in one sound. This was not a theory that Colin had made up himself. Virginia Woolf, a thoroughly respectable writer, has said as much, somewhere. Colin made a mental note to look up just where. In the meantime he revisited the idea of *the thing itself;* the object that was itself alone, and perfect. *The cherry tree is all that it does,* says Fenellosa (reference available on request). Leaves, berries, roots and blossoms, the tree stood complete in its functions, not desiring money or love. You could not have it—that much was certain, if anything was, because once you had a cherry tree in your pocket, it was not alone any more, and neither were you. All you could have was wanting it. Oh dear. Such a complicating thing, desire.

Desire. Colin knew the various forms that it could take—light-stepping, feverish, all-filling dream of air—let's shut out the daylight and meld our flesh and blood into something rich and sweet, then emerge eventually for brunch, wet-haired and blind in the afternoon sun. It was natural, between the ages of 15 and 35, to feel this way on a regular basis, once, if not four times a year. Even in the past year, Colin could not deny that he had experienced a definite physiological response to the new administrative assistant: small, dark, compact as an old-fashioned cigarette case. He overran his photocopying allocation ruthlessly during the winter session, all for the pleasure of being pistol-whipped by Tulipa Ferrari's sharp tongue.

Still, Colin shied away from the physical logistics of entanglement. He worried about his weight and the moment of displacement; if a woman should invite him to share a bath with her, for example. And of course love does not last, and does not improve, but only atrophies. Do not all the novels demonstrate it? The fever that does not bring about death or lifelong separation from one's parents abates and clears up. One only has to survive the dangerous years (15–35, as mentioned above); to build a life raft of useful things strapped together with webbing—a good pepper grinder, a modest wine collection, the complete recordings of the Beethoven string quartets, a gaseous golden retriever called Calliope—and then one is ready to ride out the tempests.

Surely there could be no harm in paying a visit to a former student and her relatives?

Colin pulled off the highway at a coffee place where rows of Harley Davidsons glittered in the sunlight, mocking him for the roads he had not taken. He straightened his waistcoat and stood as upright as possible in the lineup behind a man in black leather with fringed sleeves. *Dada's Donuts,* the place was called. He ordered a plain one.

Back on the road he drained the last drops of his coffee. It had taken two goes to get the car started. The Volvo was beginning to show its age.

"Fuck," said Colin, into the coffee cup. He was disappointed that this was the first monosyllable that came to mind, but he quite liked the hollow sound that his voice made inside the cardboard cup.

"Book," said Colin into cup, "tea." Could these words have more integrity than a word like "crappomundi," which he had once heard a student mutter while collecting her library books off the floor? The monosyllable as *the thing itself* was a silly conceit, like pitting the grunt against the drawn-out moan in a great competition to express a truth that, as the theorists had so lately discovered, no longer existed.

"Sam," said Colin.

When he arrived, the young woman in question opened the cottage door and heaven was there, on the screen porch, for the brief span it took to say that he hoped he *had the right place,* and she said *yes you do,* and she looked at him as if he were as delightful as spring blossoms under snow, and she said, *where is your bag?* and he said, *it's in the car,* and before he could prevent her she dashed away to get it.

Colin leaned against the doorframe, smiling at the insouciant rustle of the pine needles beneath her bare feet. How quickly those qualities of *samnicity* came rushing back to him: tough as a stalk, bony of finger and knee, together with his own shortness of breath at the thought that if she turned her head fast enough her ponytail might make a whistling sound in the air.

Then she took him down to the dock and it quickly became awful. Three seconds after they had been introduced, he could not recall whether Sam's stepmother's name was Myra or Myrna. Myra/Myrna gave him champagne with tiny Quebec blueberries in it to choke upon. The stepmother pointed out a grove of old growth white pine, and a boathouse that they were accustomed to rent out to a postman. In response, Colin commented on the tongues of light licking up the trunks of the cedars. After comparing the water lilies bobbing in the cove to poached eggs, he thought it better to stop.

Just beside the dock, a phrase from *As You Like It* was scored into the Canadian Shield, displacing the mossy covering that once grew there. Colin read it aloud, and as he began, he knew that all visitors to the cottage did the same thing:

And this our life, exempt from public haunt
Finds—

Samantha and Myra/Myrna chimed in,

Tongues in trees, Books in the running brooks,
Sermons in stones, and good in everything.

"It's a bit indulgent, I know," said Myra/Myrna, laughing, "but we freshen up the carving every couple of years. We have a sharp chisel for the purpose. It reminds us to be grateful. Even during bug season. Benedictions in blackflies, wisdom in weeds, magic in mosquitoes…."

Samantha took up the refrain:

"Lechery in lichen, frolics in ferns, bathos in blueberries, pathos in..."

While she chanted, she tied her hair up. Colin looked away. It was impossible to witness the movement of her shoulder blades and not to wish to make a personal measurement of the space between the lopsided bikini bow and the slight shadow it cast on the middle of her back.

Pathos in professors. He had the worst possible case of it. The cherry tree is all that it does, Sam is all that she does, did, might do. Colin attempted to focus on the stepmother instead. Myra/Myrna's skin was apricot, and her hair a darker shade. She was hearty as an apple, just as Sam was reedy as a stem.

"She's my stepmother," Sam had said on the way down to the dock, "after Dad died she brought me up, and I love her for that."

Colin summoned his most interested voice. "So, Myrna, what is your particular field of expertise within economics?"

"Myra, Colin." Sam's stepmother chided him gently, nudging his ankle with her bare foot, "and I'm in real estate."

Myra had well-tended nails, a jangle of bracelets, cropped pants. She wore a spiral toe ring in the shape of a serpent with a glistening red eye. Her look seemed to say, *Sam is twenty-four, you can go ahead and ask her.* But he could not. There are some things that you just cannot have, and if you try, you will make a fool of yourself.

"Is there a...? May I?" He waved his hand back up at the house.

"Of course, make yourself at home Professor P. The bathroom's just down the corridor from the kitchen." Myra stood up to let him past. "We'll be waiting for you."

There was a splash and the dock swayed up and down. Sam was in, her narrow form gliding under the water.

It had been a long time since Professor Pilchard had taught Shakespeare. *As You Like It*, he seemed to recall, was set in an enchanted forest where members of court fed each other strawberries and disported themselves in idleness. Sam's dock was indeed a setting for such pleasures, but something about the act of inscription bothered him. He felt that the words ought to float up like smoke from a thin-stemmed clay pipe, hang in the air, and then be off. The sermon in the stone is that everything wears away. The book in the brook is that water runs on. The engraving seemed rather, and he hated to apply the word to Sam or to her family: vulgar. *Make yourself at home Professor P.*

Relieved, Colin returned to the living room where he sat a moment in a chair covered in golden velvet with a pattern of black lozenges. His glance ranged over the objects in the room.

There he found a mixture of furniture from across the decades, unconnected by any overarching aesthetic vision except for the passage of the sun, principally a purple fun fur beanbag chair, and an enormous radiogram now functioning as a sideboard. Colin set the champagne glass down on the arm of the chair. He contemplated the bubbles that had attached themselves to the blueberries at the bottom. Perhaps *the thing itself* was not a cherry tree, but a bubble. Sooner rather than later, a bubble pops.

The professor moved his hand as if to wave the thought away, and the glass flew onto the floor, where it shattered, discharging its cargo of blueberries across the tiles.

"Oh dear," he said.

He thought about returning to the dock to confess to Myrna/Myra that he had broken one of her champagne flutes. But that would necessitate apologies and muddled groping on the floor with paper towels and the creation of shared memory—

"Do you remember the first time that I met you, you broke one of my grandmother's—"

"And you thought you would never forgive me—"

"But I did. And then one day you brought round to the house, a complete—"

Bathos in blueberries. Colin did not want shared memories with Myrna/Myra.

He ignored the broken glass on the floor and leaned back, staring upwards to where bright spots jiggled and swayed in the angles of the ceiling. Sam was down there stirring up the bay, and the jittery light on the ceiling was caused by the movement of her body in the water, but Sam was unaware of his regard; neither subject could see the other, and yet between them they had created this flickering object. Could *the thing itself* be some kind of charged space between two blind subjects? One of the greats must have already phrased the thought memorably, elegantly, in a couplet. He sent a shadowy messenger off into the archives to look for the reference.

Colin sighed. Adrift on his raft made of copper-bottomed pots and Beethoven string quartets, he became aware that he would much rather be in his office than here, risking it all in the forest, for the sake of Sam and a flicker of hope.

Fool. A monosyllable, Shakespearean, holding at once the carnal capital F, the L of a love that dithered about like light on the ceiling, and in between the puckered mouths of the supplicants. He would not be a fool.

Coward. A word of two syllables with which he could be satisfied. Associate Professor Colin Pilchard, Coward. He patted his waistcoat pocket for his keys, picked up the pigskin bag from beside the screen door, slipped outside and crept up the path towards the car, giving thanks for the uncaring silky whisper of the pine needles beneath his feet.

Vandals in Sandals

MAX WAS STILL ANNOYED with Bea for having clipped the wing mirror on the way out of the garage. The mirror hung limply, broken at the bone. Bea felt bad about it, since the van was new. She looked out at the poplar leaves spinning on their stems. She knew without hearing them that the lush sound of well-waxed summer leaves had been replaced with a clattering like rice wafers. Fall was coming and after that, nothing but snow.

"Can't we open the windows?" Bea asked, "I'd like to hear the leaves."

"Air conditioning. Better to keep them shut," said Max.

From the back seat Cammy's little brown hand appeared with an apple core.

"You can throw it out the window here, sweetie," Bea said. "It's the country."

"Don't encourage her to litter, Bea. It's all someone's frontage," said Max.

Bea looked at the maple seedlings and the crooked fence and the darkness of the firs behind.

"Okay." Bea took Cammy's applecore. "I'll save it for the compost. Where's the trash container?"

"Here." Max pressed a button and a compartment slid open. "Don't forget to get it out later," he said.

"Are we there yet?" asked Cammy.

"The agent said it was around here somewhere." Bea looked at the map again. "So we've passed Lac Perdu, right?"

"Thought you were doing the map." Max was unsmiling.

Oh give it up, she thought. *Get a grip. It's only the wing mirror.* She looked out the window again. The road curved past a stand of beeches. The layered quality of their branches seemed familiar, like hands outspread, pleading for calm.

"Slow down," she said. "I think the turnoff's back there, after the beeches. Before the dumpsters."

"Are you sure?"

"Yes I'm sure."

Max made a U-turn, and they drove back past three dumpsters overflowing with Labour Day discards. A tilting pile of tires leaned into the ragweed. Nearby, a useless sled lay in the sun, its slats warped with damp.

"Look, a sled," said Cammy. "Can I have it?"

"It's trash," said her father.

"But I could fix it," Cammy insisted.

"Look we don't have time to pick up trash for you, as well as for your mother."

"Sorry Daddy."

"Don't worry, love," said Bea. "If we find a cottage to buy we'll get you a new sled. How about that?"

The van started up the hill. With a click all the doors locked. Bea didn't like it. The van was just too much. The roadside was bright with black-eyed susans, some pure yellow and fine as stars, others rusty as old nails. Day lilies had seeded in the ditches, and tendrils of purple vetch fingered the greenery. They sped past a swampy area spiked with dead trees. A nerve in Bea's jaw tingled with recognition; she knew this road, she knew these trees. Once upon a time, a boy called Yves had shown her a heron perched high on a skeletal branch in this very swamp. Bea had been ten, spending the summer in a rented cottage with her parents.

Yves lived in the neighbouring cottage. Together, the children explored the surrounding land. Once he plucked at her sleeve to draw her attention to a young fox chasing flies on the path in front of them. Bea thought that nothing could equal the fox, but she was the first to see the weasel slipping along under the rock fall, its dark body undulating like an animated moustache. One afternoon they watched a pair of catfish herding their young about in the shallows. Yves made gestures indicating that the parents ate their babies. Bea watched the tiny wriggling commas with renewed interest. Another day she showed him a snake, run over and flat as a shoelace. The next, Yves showed her a discarded shoelace, flat and braided as a squashed snake.

Inside the cottage, Bea's parents played cards by lamplight and went to bed early. The lamps emitted a soft ball of light, not bright enough to do anything by, except, as she realized now, conceive a second child. Each morning, Bea washed the shadow of soot out of the glass chimneys. At the end of the summer, they beat out carpets, took down flypapers, pulled the curtains and drove one last time down the bumpy drive-way. Bea saw Yves out the back window. Small, he waved from the dock.

The day of the heron, they had been heading out to swim in the lake at the bottom of the hill, but when Yves reached the end of the driveway, he turned and ran uphill instead, shouting for Bea to follow. Just when she thought that she could run no more, Yves started back down the hill into the dip where the swamp pressed close to the sides of the road. Hot and sweating, they passed into a band of water-cooled air, entering a chilled land, where ghosts dwelt in the sunlight. The yellow daisies shone like stars beside the road and the heron rose up in flight. Yves and Bea flapped their arms and ran on down to swim. She kept her T-shirt on. His strong brown legs glistened when he came out of the water, wet as a salamander.

Now the road had been sealed. The day lilies still filled the ditches, although hydro workers had cut the tops off the pines to make way for cables. Max kept driving, but the road ended in a driveway leading to a summer camp and a cliff face. Bea knew that already. She had climbed there with Yves, searching for fossils.

Bea had to put her glasses on to read the words spray-painted onto the rock. She flushed and looked at the map. *Petit Hibou, ça m'empêche pas de continuer à t'aimer. Yves.*

"Funny name for a girl," said Max. "Old Yves sounds a bit desperate. It's quite the custom round here to proclaim your love on a rock. Remember all those names on the way up to La Tuque?"

"What does it say, Daddy?"

"It says that he won't stop loving her. Little vandal."

"What's a vandal?"

"A person who wears sandals and writes on walls."

"Vandals in sandals."

"Yes, and Goths in socks."

"Vandals in sandals and Goths in socks, Goths in thocks. Thocks in Goths."

"Do you think we could open a window *now?*" Bea's voice was sharp. The brittle sound of the late summer leaves came to her. The locusts roared in the banks.

"Looks like this is a dead end," said her husband. "I guess your hunch was wrong."

"I guess it was, I'm sorry," she said.

"No problemo, it's a nice day to be out for a drive, isn't it Cammy? In our sandals in the new vandal."

"Vandal sandal candle dandle." Cammy launched into the rest of the alphabet.

The words fell like light blows. Bea endured them all. Surely, she thought, it won't always be like this. They turned and drove back down the hill, past the swamp, past the empty branch where the heron had been, past the daisies, and back to the dumpsters at the bottom of the road.

Where the Corpse
Weed Grows

ISABELLA'S SKIRT BRUSHED through the ferns at the side of the track, collecting burrs, hooked seeds, the hem dusted yellow by the furry tongues of pollen-bearing plants. She had found the skirt in a costumes sale. Now what she needed was an old crone (she consulted the back of the park brochure) of Atikamekw ancestry, someone bent over, wise in the ways of plants and their healing powers, devoted to helping true seekers like herself. In the absence of a crone, the woman in the ticket booth said she would find a park warden at a hut called Espérance.

Isabella wrinkled up her nose. She had so wanted to feel the quest with the whole of her body; to cross a boggy patch, sensing the step and suck of waterlogged ground, tripping on rocks and roots as she hunted for the plants. But the track resisted her. It remained gravelly and dry.

A horsefly that had been buzzing around her went very quiet and Isabella hoped that it was not caught in her hair. She was beginning to regret not having removed the hair extensions after the show closed. They were much longer strands than her natural hair, tinted deep green, and now they seemed heavy and hot. The director wanted his Ophelia to look like she had already been floating in the river for a while, because he said they were all ghosts, doomed from the beginning, and no one in the audience could pretend to be ignorant of how *Hamlet* turned out, so the audience, through their expectation, became complicit with the drive of tragedy. Whenever he said *complicit* (and he said it often) he passed his hand over the shaved crown of his head. The director was brilliant; Isabella adored him. She did anything that he asked her to do, anything at all.

Isabella was always at a loose end between shows, which was why a personal quest seemed so attractive. It began with a pamphlet from the health-food store. The pamphlet described a herbal product called Elcarim, proclaiming its value as a potent cure for cancer. In the 1930s, a nurse had received the recipe from an Indian healer. She mixed and bottled huge batches of the stuff with which she healed the sick across the province. The pamphlet listed the plants used in the formula, describing how the nurse had given up the recipe in a sworn affidavit, extracted on her deathbed. *Sworn affidavit.* The phrase was so romantic. Isabella wanted to be that nurse.

She decided to gather the ingredients and prepare the Elcarim herself. First she needed a trug to lay the plants in, and then there would be boiling and steeping, leaving the mixture in the dark, straining, reheating, and finally offering her mother a cup of the liquid, which would surely taste bitter and earthy. Honey, perhaps she could add honey, if Moira needed a sweetener.

Isabella made the preparations necessary to spend a weekend away with Moira, booking a motel that she could not afford, hauling her down the stairs and into the car, tugging the seatbelt tight around her bulk. Moira was collapsed on the couch at the motel now, her body hidden in the great flowered folds of her dress, the non-paralysed side of her face working with effort at the donuts in the box, one eyelid tugged downwards by the frozen waterfall of her face. After the potion had been prepared, the Elcarim would pour through the massive body in a thin stream, for good or for harm working its way along the veins. Her mother would nod, give thanks for such a dedicated and loving daughter. And then she would die.

Isabella stopped short. She had not expected this thought to occur to her. Before her, in the middle of the road, as if dropped from above, lay a shrew caught in the surprise of death, its paws in the air, its whiskers a fan of dewdrops. She crouched down to look at it. Patches of skin shone through the short grey fur gathered with moisture. Her mother's scalp showed in the same way when she washed her hair. Under the shrew's pointed snout a tongue like a pink grain of rice stuck out above teeth that were sharp and dirty brown.

Once upon a time, Isabella's mother had been Moira Delacourt, the lounge singer. Never a beauty, her charms lay in her voice, husky with cigarette smoke. Moira's attentions flew about like thistledown. She delighted in everything, forever exclaiming, taking people by the arm, walking a few steps with them. A bee, she went from flower to flower. The acidic tongue she saved for home, and for Isabella.

What recipe, what formula had Moira followed to bring Isabella up? None, just a selfish kind of blundering, until surprised by age and illness, she found that she had to rely more than she had imagined on her grown child. And Isabella's life? Not much to tell really, theatre school, work as an extra, a time of famine, bit parts, a lucky break, musicals that toured summer festivals and Shakespeare plays in parks, lovers of both sexes who came and went on the tide of the theatre seasons.

Isabella straightened up, and hurried on leaving the shrew behind. The roadway led uphill under maple trees that leaned in overhead making an enchanted tree cathedral, the ideal place for a wedding procession of children bearing poles tied with ribbons and hoops entwined with roses. She smiled to think how those children would dance and sing, making way for the happy couple.

Espérance was a large log cabin with a roof of shingles that had blackened with age. A sign on the door requested that Isabella take off her boots and respect the spirit of the place. Isabella put her head in at the door and looked around.

"Bonjour, hello?" she called out.

A moose head regarded her from high up beside a field-stone fireplace of immense proportions but the reply came from behind her, from a young man holding an armful of firewood.

"One minute," he said.

He brushed past her skirt, crossed the room and knelt down to stack the wood beside the fireplace. She watched him from behind, admiring his buttocks in the khaki shorts. He was not the crone she needed, but maybe he was better: a shape-changer, a thief or an angel. He was cute, whatever he was, small and slender, with yellow brown curls, a light beard, and round glasses that reflected the panes in the window and the plane of light that was the lake beyond.

They shook hands, so formal and polite. His name was Pascal. Breathless, because it was such a relief to talk to someone, she told him the story, how her mother was a retired jazz singer taken first with paralysis of the face and now with cancer, how this potion, this Elcarim offered a cure, how there was a recipe, written down in a sworn affidavit, and if he could show her what these plants looked like, she could make some herself.

He raised his eyebrows. "You are not the first person to ask me about this Elcarim. Just buy it off the Internet."

"Can't you at least show me what the plants look like?"

He sighed. "Okay, but you cannot take the plant. It is a National Park."

"I know. Hands off the pristine wilderness."

"What is on your list?" He started putting on his boots.

"Burdock root," she said.

"Ah, Burdock," he said, jabbing the end of lace through each eyelet in turn, "Cockle Button, Clot-Bur, T'orny Burr, 'appy Major, Love Leave." His French accent made the most prosaic English names chime like bells. "You have some seed pod stuck to your dress, but you want the root. They assist in the elimination of the free radical."

Dress, he said dress. Isabella looked at him, fascinated. He was one of those men who do not know the difference between a dress and a skirt.

"What else?" he asked.

"Sheep sorrel," she said.

"Look beside your car at le parking. Small flower, red. Next?"

"Some kind of rhubarb."

"So is it the Indian rhubarb *(Rheum officinale)* or the Turkish rhubarb *(Rheum palmatum)?*"

"I don't know," said Isabella.

"Listen to me, mademoiselle: order it off the internet," said Pascal.

"I just thought it would be more natural to make it. It's supposed to be a miracle cure, and I don't want to buy a miracle mail order."

"So you think a miracle is *naturel?* Let her die. This is *naturel.* What do you do for a living?" he asked.

"I'm an actor."

"*Tabernouche,*" he muttered.

"What difference does that make?" said Isabella. "Are you this nasty to everyone who asks you for help? I'm doing this for my mother, you know." She opened her eyes as wide as she could, looked up at him from under the heavy burden of her dark green hair.

"Excuse me," he said finally. "I am very busy today. I have to check some permit of fishing at Lac Parker. Come with me. I will show you some plant."

Pascal took the track up the hill in short quick strides, pushing his mountain bike in front of him. Isabella picked up her skirts and hurried behind, keeping her eyes on his calf muscles. *My cherub,* she might call him, if he were to become her lover, if he were to leave the forest, come get a job waiting tables in the big city. She wanted him for his youth, for the hard thin torso beneath the skin. His skin would be satiny. There would be a line where the tan stopped.

She began to perspire. Now she was having a real experience, surging onwards in the wake of Pascal making his way up the hill. Why, there were even berries beside the track, three on a narrow stem; globes of bright dark blue like the sky in a storybook. They were passing a spot where the rocks hung over the river and you could slide in under the ledge where the water foamed alongside. You could scrub it down, get rid of any slime that might grow in the shadows.

"Look," he said, pointing to the base of a birch tree where a white plant was growing out of the leaf litter.

"What's that?" she asked.

"Indian pipe plant."

"Is it in the Elcarim recipe?"

"No. Look. It is a plant without chlorophyll."

The pipe plant grew singly and in clumps, not tall, its head drooping over in a bell. The whole plant was white, not clean white like paper, not translucent like cooked fish, but ghastly white. It had thin waxy stems, frilled about like a toadstool, and at the opening of the bell, where a bee might land, there was a black rosette, puckered like a tiny dark mouth.

Pascal was looking hard at her.

"Now ask me why I'm showing you this," he said.

Isabella asked. She was good at taking directions.

"Why are you showing me this?"

"Because it looks dead, but it is alive," he said. "We call it Corpse Weed. The living dead of nature. You see? Death grows, it lives with you. Go to your mother, sit with her, and listen to her."

"But I can't stand it," said Isabella.

Once, long before theatre school, before high school even, at the age of 11, she took up her mother's guitar and began to play, thinking to please Moira with a song that she had made up herself. Moira came into the room, drink in hand. She sat down to listen. Part way through the second verse, Moira stood up and carefully placed her drink down on the coffee table.

"You have made a mistake," she said in a quiet, cold voice. Before Isabella could ask how Moira knew that when she had written the song herself, Moira grabbed the guitar out of Isabella's hands, and swung it, smashing its back against the stone wall of the living room.

"I said you have made a mistake," she said again, without raising her voice. "I am the singer, not you."

The corpse plant was stupid and ugly and the colour of an old dog turd. Isabella wanted to crush it under her heel. Hopelessness crept through her skull like mist, hung like a damp aura about the bright vision of her mother, once Moira Delacourt the lounge singer, now spread out upon the couch at the motel, aggressively eating donuts to show the world that she could still do something. Isabella did not especially want her mother to live or die, what she wanted was a different mother.

"How come you know so much, Mr Pascal Park Warden?" she said.

"Excuse me?"

"I said how come you know so much?"

"Mother, sister, breast cancer. Okay?"

Her mouth refused to work. She could not think what to say.

"Okay," he said, looking off up the hill. "So now I am going to check the permit of fishing. You know where to go? Down the hill, along the lake."

Her mouth unfroze long enough to twitch out the words of thanks for his time.

"No problem. *Bonne chance* with that miracle." He disappeared up the hill on his bike.

Isabella took off her skirt, suddenly sick of it, and bunched it up in front of her. Barelegged she started down the path, kicking at the brown stones as she went, reciting Ophelia's lines in a sulky voice. *He is dead and gone, lady, He is dead and gone.*

She was surprised by the tinging of bells ahead. Two men on mountain bikes were making their way up the track, ringing as they went. They looked at Isabella's legs and with some enthusiasm announced that they had seen a bear, so she ought to make noise as she went. Show tunes, they suggested. Show tunes? Isabella could do show tunes.

She knew it looked out of the ordinary: a woman with dark green hair emerging from among the trees, her legs scratched by briars and thorns, belting out that the sun would come out tomorrow; singing to keep the bears at bay.

The Frog

CARL COULD NOT HAVE been out of sight for more than seconds before Robyn could no longer hear the sticks cracking under his sandals. The sound of the boy's movements had blended into the overhead rush of the leaves and the rustling of the river water around the rocks. Robyn sat very still on the riverbank. A lone maple leaf spooled past in the current. It was silly to panic on a Sunday morning.

"Let's cut through the trees here. The portage trail must be over the hill."

Robyn's older sister Sandrine had made the suggestion not five minutes ago. They were supposed to be rock-hopping down the river to the next lake. Robyn knew that the river would arrive at the lake and so would the portage trail, but that did not mean that the portage trail would follow the river. She didn't want to cut through the trees.

There was already a woman missing in the national park. Yesterday they had seen her picture on a poster at the gate. She was older than Robyn, 33, 5'6," 140 pounds, with pale curly hair. She was last seen wearing a green polar fleece. Her mountain bike was silver with yellow panniers. The woman did not have the appearance of someone who wanted to leave life behind. She looked happy enough to stay with the person who had taken her photograph. There must have been an accident.

The water flowing beside Robyn made a hollow gollop as it fell from a pitcher-shaped scoop of stone. Perhaps the photograph was old. Perhaps the woman did want to be lost. Robyn could not remember her name.

The day had begun well enough, fresh and bright, with only the slightest hint of fall coolness in the wind that blew the hair back from their foreheads while they ate their oatmeal. They had camped the previous night at the head of the lake, and now they hoisted the cooler up high beyond the reach of animals, stowed their gear in the tent and set off.

Where the river left the lake the rocks were large and encrusted with algae. The morning sun winked off the tepid pools between them. Carl walked along the riverbank, startling a large green frog back into the water. They all crouched down to admire its strong kick.

"A frog knows where it wants to go," said Carl. It took ten minutes of effort, but he caught the frog in a net and put it in his collecting jar where it scrabbled at the plastic sides, its scythe-like swimming toes still kicking.

Robyn wanted to return the frog to its habitat, but Carl was determined to let the frog go at the next lake.

"It will start a new colony there," he said.

Sandrine went first, leaping from rock to rock down the middle of the river. Her boots had a good grip. She did not care if she got wet. Robyn and Carl idled along the river's edge, stooping under branches, swinging around the up-thrust ruddy trunks of the cedars, and squatting to examine fat caterpillars that had fallen off the maple trees into the pools. Under an overhanging bank Robyn found four toadstools arranged like orange candles on a cupcake of moss. To Robyn the day felt as special as a birthday. She was showing the toadstools to Carl when Sandrine turned around and shouted back up the river at her.

"Robyn, come on." Sandrine lengthened the syllables in a flat sing-song way.

"Don't get your knickers in a twist, Sardine," said Robyn under her breath. Carl looked at his mother, surprised.

"Sardine?" he said.

June and Jonathan Cleghorn had two daughters: Sandrine and Robyn. Sandrine was the athletic one and Robyn was the younger one.

Nothing deterred Sandrine. In March, all through high school, Sandrine was up before dawn, skiing out over the back field until the sky turned pink and Robyn appeared on the back porch, her windmilling arms the signal that breakfast was ready. Then Sandrine would jump and turn to halt, the hardened snow crystals skittering out behind her. No matter what the season, when you hugged Sandrine, you could feel the cold air in a cloud about her cheekbones.

For the last six years, Sandrine had spent the summer months of the Northern hemisphere working as a Nordic ski instructor in the South Island of New Zealand. Robyn had seen photos of the apricot sunset behind the mountain tops, but she still could not imagine Nordic skiing above the treeline. It was just like Sandrine to find a previously un-thought of way to perform a regular physical activity. All she had to do was go to the other side of the world to do it. This year, rain had ruined the southern ski season. Sandrine had not been home three days before she decided to take Robyn and Carl on a camping trip.

Robyn had no need to make grand trans-Pacific migrations. She lived what she thought of as a kitchen-centred life. She located clean gym shorts for Carl, she used up the rhubarb at the back of the fridge, she worked shifts at Clifton's Greek & Italian Restaurant and she ferried Carl and his cello to music lessons.

Robyn was always amazed by the way that people without children appeared to have no idea about the elastic skein of responsibility created by motherhood. Dashing about the globe, people without children just slid in and out of other people's kitchencentred lives like, and here Robyn could not think of a word that was not vaguely slippery. Whatever it was, it was frustrating. People without children even had time to find the words for things.

Occasionally, Robyn would remember that ten years ago she too was a person without children. Usually her next thought would be *and that's how I got pregnant.*

*

Robyn sat on the riverside in the wavering forest light.

"Come on Robyn," Carl called out from the other side of the river.

Robyn looked at Carl's strong knees and ankles. He was standing on one leg holding onto a cedar branch for balance, his collecting jar in the other hand. Whatever had happened to *Come on Mom?*

Sandrine started off into the forest. Carl, drawn by the charm of her energy, turned his back and bounded up the bank after his aunt, pushing his way through the spindly lower branches of the firs until he disappeared over the top of the incline.

So, Carl had left her; Carl was nearly ten. Adolescence could not be far off. Earlier in the week Robyn had heard him practising his cello against her. He was in his bedroom with the door shut, playing minor scales, all the way up and over the extended penultimate interval, but stopping short of the top. He knew that she would be listening at the bottom of the stairs; he was not going to give her the satisfaction of the last note.

Robyn looked at a black spray of weed that floated in the current. She turned her mouth down. She did not move from her rock. All she could think was: *I'm the mother. I should get to decide whether we cut across.*

In order to tell them that she was not coming she would have to go far enough into the woods to be able to see them; it would be the same as following them. Sandrine might stop and call out, but she would not turn back. Robyn would be expected to follow because Robyn always did follow Sandrine, and because Carl was there.

"I don't want to," she said aloud, but there was no one to hear. She stood up and began picking her way downstream over the rocks.

Carl's father had been a guitarist in a band called The Chokers. He had been Robyn's chiaroscuro lover for one week only; appearing golden out of the darkness of a basement bar. The unexpected pregnancy had terminated Robyn's studies in art history. She had returned home to her parents' brick house at Stonehaven where she took on the life that was expected of her.

In Stonehaven there was not much room for words like chiaroscuro. Clifton's Greek and Italian Restaurant served pizza for the boys and salads for the girls, with the olives and feta on the side, since it was Stonehaven after all. Robyn was one of the girls, a group of women who plated the house salads, served the meals and scrubbed off the tomato splatters that the chef baked onto the stovetop.

Clifton Smith, who owned the restaurant, was the son of a former mayor of Stonehaven. He was built like a pyramid with a good solid base. In the winter he wore big mittens and a thick charcoal peacoat zipped against the cold. He paid attention to the quality of the vinaigrette and he disliked salt stains on the carpet at the door.

"I'll leave it to you girls to divvy up the tasks," he would say if there was a special event to cater for. *Divvy, savvy, nifty;*

these were Clifton's words. Robyn had been seeing Clifton for two years now. Their most recent date had been to the outlook at the meteor crater. He had brought leftover stuffed vine leaves and a thermos of coffee. Together they looked out at the trees, which was all that could be seen of the remnants of the cosmic event, unless you went up in a plane. Clifton had his hand high up on her thigh and Robyn was holding her travel mug up to her aching wisdom teeth. *Perhaps I could make a nifty wife after all,* she had thought, looking out the window.

Last night, after Carl had rolled himself up, grub-like, in his sleeping bag with a book and a flashlight, Sandrine washed the dishes while Robyn dried them, trying to make a stack without having them all topple over in the dust.

"How's Cliff?" asked Sandrine.

"He's fine," Robyn spoke without looking up. "Business is good."

Sandrine said nothing for a moment.

"Look at me," she said finally.

"What?" said Robyn. "There's nothing with Cliff."

"Oh I know there's nothing really wrong with Cliff. We all know Cliff."

Robyn thought of the former mayor's son moving through his restaurant, resting his large hands on the shoulders of men who as primary-school boys had dropped his raincoat in the urinal and pissed on it. There was nothing wrong with Clifton, but Sandrine had a knack for making everything that Robyn did seem wrong.

When Sandrine wasn't in town, Robyn was content with her life in Stonehaven. Only the shape of the main street bothered her. Whenever she left the restaurant, she could not suppress a rise in her spirits in response to the uphill turn in the road. Over the bridge the road went, before curving to the right and starting upwards, past city hall with its silver pepper shaker top, then onwards, and out of sight. The road promised so much, and yet by the time Robyn had crossed the bridge and glanced at the discarded white ware dumped under the willows, she could see as well as know that there was nothing beyond city hall except Zeebe's Auto Parts, Lula's XXX Videos and a handful of drafty brick houses with short concrete paths. She was annoyed that she still fell for the lure of the road.

If you got lost in a national park in August you would have to be disciplined to catch and dry enough frogs, berries and snails for the winter months. Carl and Robyn had discussed eating frogs earlier in the day. A frog might be best served marinated and wrapped in a leaf, or swimming in butter like the snails on the menu at the restaurant. Robyn suggested that Carl ask Clifton when he came to dinner on Wednesday. Carl said nothing. He tended to slide off to his room when Clifton was around.

The river narrowed into a high rocky gulley where the sides had been hollowed out by spring floods. Robyn was glad that it was late summer and the water level was low. The sound of voices drifted down through the foliage high over her head. Two people were singing the chorus to the Gypsy Rover. *He whistled and he sang and the green woods rang, for he won the heart of a lady.* She recognized Carl's voice. He would be a musician like his father. Robyn had avoided telling him about The Chokers. She had never wanted Carl to think of his father as an itinerant player.

So her sister had been right, the trail was just through the woods and at that point it did run parallel with the river. Perhaps Robyn ought to have followed them along the portage trail after all. It would be easier going than the river. Portage was a comforting word, close to potage, the thick vegetable soup that Clifton served at the restaurant in the winter months. She wondered if she would ever find herself following Clifton along a portage trail, Coleman lamp in one hand, cooler in the other, two paddles under her arms, with her husband turned toucan under the fibreglass hull of a canoe.

Ahead there was a bridge. Robyn slipped into the ferny shadows beneath it. She had thought she might call out to surprise them, but she found herself unwilling to give up her temporary camouflage. She wondered why they could not see her. Perhaps they did not expect to see her. Once confirmed in her hunch, Sandrine would have forgotten Robyn's reluctance to leave the river. They had not even thought to look back.

Sandrine and Carl crossed over the bridge. Through the slats and the chicken wire Robyn could see the soles of Sandrine's boots and beside them Carl's sandals. They were walking side by side. *Sandrine wants a child.* The thought had not occurred to Robyn before. Their song faded into the woods. If Robyn did not come back, Sandrine would make sure that Carl got his practice done. She would see to the gym gear.

Beyond the narrow straits, the river bed fanned out into a sunlit marsh of reeds and nests, of sedge and low growing myrtle. Robyn stepped from one clump of cotton bushes and pitcher plants to another, trying to avoid the down-sucking mud between. Mosquitoes swarmed about her face and arms. She crouched low, moving crabwise, grabbing at the rotten logs that lay on mossy mats of raspberry and green stars. Robyn felt like an escapee. She half-expected to hear dogs baying in pursuit.

Robyn had also been right. The portage trail and the river diverged tracks at the marsh. Sandrine and Carl stood on the shore almost three hundred metres further along the water's edge. They had their hands on their hips and were looking around. To get back to them Robyn would have to cross a cove of water lilies and pickerel weed.

She'd had enough of the marsh and she moved out into the shallow water eagerly, wading until she tripped on a submerged log and found herself lying in the water. After that she crawled along on her hands through the water lilies, surprised by how quickly she got used to the casual slimy brush of the underwater stems and the sharp pricking of submerged branches. Among the water lilies she stopped and looked around. The water was sun-warmed and clear, the bottom silted and silky. Some lily pads had flipped over, showing their scarlet undersides. Right side up, their tops were a hardened waxy green touched not just by dragonflies but also by a host of smaller insects. Every now and then she encountered the upraised golden fist of a water lily yet to flower.

Robyn kicked her legs out behind her and thought of the golden rims of the frog's eyes. *Amphibian;* that was the word she could not remember, that was the word that she wanted to describe the way a person without children moves through the world. *I am an amphibian.* Her jaws opened and closed over the words like a frog's. She could see her sister standing on the sandy beach ahead of her. Carl was bending over his empty collecting jar. Soon she would have to stand up and make herself visible once more. She did not want to, but she would.

Mrs Viebert's Prognostication

LIKE A PLAYING CARD with twelve diamonds on it, Mrs Viebert possessed all the normal parts of ladies, but in greater quantities. From his hiding place behind the purple clematis, his pockets full of sandwich crusts, nine-year-old Norman spied her approaching his house on her piggy trotter heels, patting the back of her hair as she came, calling to her daughter, Baby Viebert, to come along. Mrs Viebert was as magnificent as the figurehead on the prow of a ship, and the rose-scented air of Palmerston North parted graciously before her.

While their mothers played canasta in the company of Mr and Mrs Goring from next door, Norman and Baby Viebert filled the birdbath with puddings made of bark and petals and leaves. After they had eaten their fill, they used their spittle to attach rose pricks to their noses. Thus transformed, the two rhinoceroses stalked the shrubbery looking for Germans. Usually they rescued Baby's big brother Cyril from a snake-filled pit on the compost heap of North Africa, where the second New Zealand Division under General Freyberg had been holding out against Rommel for a week on a diet of grapefruit rinds and potato peelings.

Carrying wounded Cyril and weakened General Freyberg on their backs, the wild animals circled the house, occasionally pausing to listen at the open window. The murmuring voices of the card players did not concern them; the sound they anticipated was the squeaking wheel on the tea trolley as Norman's mother pushed it towards the rosewood table in the front room. As Norman no longer had a father, there was no one to come with a can of oil to squirt away the squeak. Of course there was Uncle Stewart, but he was not to be trusted, being naturally the kind of man who drips oil on the carpet.

On the trolley were cups and saucers with a pattern of rosebuds, a silver teapot, and a plate of squashed pea and black pepper sandwiches with the crusts cut off, the line of filling bright as lawn clippings. The lower shelf carried the double-tiered cake stand bearing a nutmeg and apple cake barely dusted with icing sugar. Rhinoceroses no longer, Norman and Baby hurried to wash their hands in the birdbath. There might be cake for good children with clean fingers.

The combined stimuli of canasta and nutmeg brought on the fleeting visions that Mrs Viebert called her prognostications. Not for Mrs Viebert the watery ways of the teacup or the drama of tarot. Her visions came with the satisfactory click of a well-sanded drawer shutting. At any rate, some time during 1941, Mrs Viebert looked out the window at the children lurking in the undergrowth, dabbed her fingertips on a napkin embroidered with flowers and wrote something on a card that she found in her handbag, together with Norman's name.

Widowed in the early months of the war, Norman's mother was no longer the woman to hold fate back from her son. She tucked the card inside an envelope and gave it to him at bedtime.

"This is yours," she said, "from Mrs Viebert. Mind it, and keep it safe."

Norman held the envelope close to his chest and stared up at the ceiling.

"I have to fly to New Zealand," Norman announced to the assembled staff at the Montreal eye clinic where he worked. "My Uncle Stewart is on his last legs."

In truth, Uncle Stewart had not only lost both legs to diabetes, he had also died in 1979. There was not much reason to lie about it; Norman was quite entitled to take a holiday. Furthermore, Norman's New Zealand relations, both the quick and the dead, were as distant to his Canadian colleagues' thinking as fruit flies. However, Norman felt that a degree of preparation was in order for the only act of mythic proportions that he would ever perform. Telling a lie seemed a reasonable start.

Norman flew out of Vancouver on Sunday, keeping his eyes fixed on the screen that showed a digital plane inching its way out over the Pacific Ocean. Once again he pulled the envelope out of his pocket and looked at it. Time had mottled the paper until it resembled the backs of Norman's hands, but the words written on it remained unchanged: Mrs Viebert's Prognostication. For the hundredth, perhaps the two-hundredth time in his life he opened the envelope and pulled out the playing card inside it. As he always did, he looked first at the picture on the back of the card: a swooning gypsy-wild, sky-tumbled Icarus, succoured by lonely mermaids whose dark auburn hair, so tastefully arranged, had stimulated his earliest adolescent fantasies. Now Norman wondered how any artist could make falling out of the sky seem an attractive option. He turned the card over and looked at the other side. It was a two of diamonds, a wild card, the kind that froze the canasta pack, calling a temporary halt to the ordinary life of the game. The card no longer smelled of the fruitcakey darkness of Mrs Viebert's handbag but the message on it was still legible: *Norman: look sharp. Monday, August 27th, 2001.*

In the 1940s, August 27th, 2001 had been as unimaginable as a Monday on the moon, but the date had loomed over Norman, squashing the more ridiculous of his adolescent impulses, keeping him safe in case he was bound for glory. A career in optometry had not left much room for mortal accident. He spent his days in a brown-walled windowless room posing questions about floating specks and numbers hidden in patterns. He had been meticulous about oil changes and snow tires, and while his marriage lasted, Aspen had proved to be a wife who was careful with her hair and not prone to credit-card debt. Indeed, the greatest risk that Norman had taken was to leave his mother and New Zealand far behind and emigrate to Canada.

Once, there had been a before and an after this date, but as middle-age came and went, Norman began to realize that it was far more likely to be the date for a cardiac arrest or being squashed by a butter truck than a date marked by Olympian achievement. Indeed, Norman had come to fear that time's form was not equally divided like an hourglass, but bottomless, like a funnel with no end. Norman could see himself arriving at Monday, August 27th, 2001, but after that he could not see very much.

An air stewardess had given him the idea that the day might be avoided altogether. Not long after his divorce, Norman found himself seated on a plane beside a man in an open-necked golf shirt. The air stewardess was very pretty and the open-necked man had asked her how she kept her looks. She replied that on every long-haul flight she missed a day in crossing the dateline, and it all added up. With a practised wink and a startling mewing sound she passed on to Norman, asking him if he would like coffee or tea. Tea, please, he had said, looking up at her smooth skin and wondering.

After Norman decided to skip the day that fate had appointed him, he organized the slow demise of Uncle Stewart through a series of postcards addressed to himself, followed by a message from a payphone, in which he regretfully informed himself, using a fake Scottish accent, that Uncle Stewart was in his final days of decline. He enjoyed these preparations and over the course of a year read each postcard aloud to the receptionist at the eye clinic, receiving her waves of sympathy with dutiful gravity.

Uncle Stewart would not have liked Norman's making use of him in this way. If he'd been alive, he might have reminded

Norman of a certain wartime evening at the kitchen table, playing Smash the Nazi Navy. Norman was watching Uncle Stewart pencil in the position of his fleet. By lining up the checks on his uncle's shirt cuff with the lines on the grid of the Smash the Nazi Navy notepad, Norman could guess where Uncle Stewart had placed his battle ships.

"You're a clever wee chap, Norm," said Uncle Stewart, after Norman sank three submarines in Uncle Stewart's North Sea. Then he clipped Norman over the ear. "But no one likes a cheat."

In the case of Mrs Viebert's prognostication, Norman did not think he was cheating. He considered himself to be reducing the odds, just in case Mrs Viebert was right. After they took her away it turned out that she had almost predicted the Tangiwai rail disaster of 1953.

It was getting late. The remains of Norman's in-flight peppered steak and his neighbour's leafy vegetarian option had been removed, the steward had passed by with tea and coffee, the stewardess had prepared the cabin for night-time. Norman rotated his ankles. He made his way to the bathroom where he felt a touch of regret that his life might soon be over and he had not smoked and he had not followed carnal impulses in aeroplane bathrooms. All he had done was dispose of his bodily refuse with a blue frozen sucking snort, and then wash up, wiping the hand basin for the convenience of the next traveller. He had made sure his will was in order; he had left a letter for Aspen in the fruit bowl. He thought she should know, in case his act of evasion should fail. She had always accused him of being secretive. Well, if he never returned, she could at least feel satisfied that she had been right.

Fortunately or unfortunately, Norman had failed to calculate that at 11:30 PM on Sunday August 26th, 2001, the plane would come down to refuel in Tahiti. With the rest of the passengers he was forced to file off into the amniotic warmth of the night, shuddering at the thought of what might lie ahead. Beside a lighted doorway, three coral-clad ukulele players set up a swaying tinkling thread of sound that followed him into the linoleum limbo of the airport lounge.

Norman surveyed the available seats and chose one equidistant from a podgy woman in ripped shorts cowering behind a bank of tropical plants, and a woman knitting. The knitter was wearing sunglasses perched on top of her head. Norman took a second look at her, wondering what she wanted with sunglasses at midnight. He felt a strong urge to lean forward and murmur to her that wearing them on her head like that would stretch the hinges.

Around him the air was full of the rustle of people waiting, anticipating arrival, or regretful of all that had been left behind. Tapping at their cell phones, they called out of the darkness into other time zones, chewing and twitching, crossing and re-crossing their legs. If Norman sat quite still, kept his eyes on the floor and made no contact with anyone, perhaps, just perhaps, he would be safe.

The alarm on Norman's watch began beeping. Monday, August 27th, 2001 had arrived. Heart beating against his plaid shirt, he wiped his forehead with his handkerchief and looked up at the scene around him. A couple beside the bank machine were necking like gannets, their camera straps clattering against each other, the flowers on their leis crumpling under the pressure. The hot perfume of crushed flowers reminded him of the yellow roses that once threatened to bring down the fence in his mother's garden. His mind was filled with a vision of himself as nine-year-old Norman fighting off the storm troopers hidden in the flax bush. He was wearing new shorts, Stand Fast Gentleman Drill, with silver buckles at the waist.

"Bombs away!" he had shouted, leaping off the front step, dropping and rolling past Baby Viebert towards the ngaio tree beside the gate. A wood pigeon, startled into evacuation by the attack, moved off, carving musical swoops in the air. While Norman stalked around the flax bush, Baby Viebert frowned over some rose petals that she was arranging in regiments on the path. Could that have been the day on which he had received the playing card from Mrs Viebert?

As an optometrist, Norman had spent decades studying weak vision, asking clients about relative lens strengths, measuring, correcting, and getting it right. Likewise he had often peered at his own past, trying to recall just when he had received Mrs Viebert's prognostication, for that could make all the difference to the outcome. Try as he might, Norman could not remember whether it was triumphant twelve-diamond Mrs Viebert who had foreseen his future, or her later and much longer lasting incarnation, Poor Gladys. He felt like his more dithery clients, who could not tell which lens was stronger, who talked themselves out of what they knew they once saw, and whom he secretly despised.

Cyril Viebert died of dysentery in May 1941, in a camp twelve miles south of Cairo. He had recently turned nineteen. Norman remembered standing in the backyard looking at a pot with a burned-out bottom just after the news came through. His mother was off comforting Poor Gladys and Uncle Stewart had been trying to be useful in the kitchen. Norman was still wearing drill shorts and his knees were cold. In similar weather Cyril Viebert's blond rugby thighs used to redden like sausages. After Norman sniffed the burned-out pot he trotted off to the front of the house. The yellow roses were all gone, but the purplish green feijoas were ripe upon the vine and Norman lobbed several at Rommel's Afrikakorps on behalf of Cyril Viebert.

Mrs Viebert stopped coming to canasta parties. She became Poor Gladys, answering her front door with her hair in disarray and her eyes red and puffed out. While his mother visited Poor Gladys, Norman waited in the garden. He made Baby Viebert eat leaves off the pepper bush hedge, and the heat on her tongue made Baby's eyes water, which was good, because she was Norman's prisoner, and it was right that she should know it. Above them the cabbage tree leaves cut slots in the sky with their cold dense blades.

Not long after space men began to speak to Poor Gladys through the radiogram they came and took her away. Then Uncle Stewart began to say *feeding flies for Tiny Freyberg*. He said it with a pretend Texan accent that he had heard on the radio. *Feedin' flahs fer Tahny Frahberg.* Sometimes Uncle Stewart could not stop saying things.

In 1951 General Freyberg became Baron Freyberg of Wellington and of Munstead in the County of Surrey. Nobody knew what became of Baby Viebert.

Norman found himself staring at the woman knitting. Orange and yellow, purple and flamingo, she had a hundred colours. One side of her knitting bristled with strands that looped and twisted and hung untrimmed. She dropped one strand, picked up another, twisted it in, and knitted on, frowning over her work. Her silver bird's nest of hair was held up by the sunglasses and a crab-like pincer high up at the back of her head. In her orange shirt, loose green trousers, sandals and a long loop of shells she looked at home in the tropical night.

A flame-coloured ball of wool dropped from her lap, rolling out over the linoleum towards Norman's foot. Without thinking he picked it up and wound it back towards her. The woman took the ball from him with a nod; her dense brown eyes studied him, without smiling. The humidity had made her hair start out in tendrils at her forehead. She finished her row and turned the knitting. Now he could see the hourglass pattern of inverted triangles forming and the diamonds in between.

They were paging Norman. This is what you get if you pay extra to fly first class to the other side of the world. They care that you are aboard, in your seat, reducing the odds. The knitting woman looked up at him again and there was energy in her glance. She made a movement with her mouth as if she were about to speak. Norman grimaced and looked away. He had made long preparations to escape this day. It was not a time for new acquaintances. He hurried away towards the gate, away from Monday, August 27th, towards Tuesday, August 28th. His shoes squeaked, resisting the linoleum.

About the time that the plane crossed the dateline, a sudden jolt of turbulence shook Norman out of his half-sleep. Norman sat up and looked at the digital plane on the screen in front of him. He had done it. He had managed to evade all but three hours of Monday, August 27th, 2001. He was not *feedin' flies*. All he had seen was a couple kissing in a tropical crush, all he had done was wind up a woman's ball of wool.

The lovers. The knitter. The figures collided in his head. All these years of waiting and he had failed to see what had been clear to Mrs Viebert both in her prime and in her grief. Now Norman struggled to reach Baby Viebert across the gap of sixty years, with her eyes so dark that the pupils were almost invisible, her hair long since turned to a mass of silvery tendrils like the pollen bearing innards of the roses that she used to pull apart. Had she not looked up when his name was paged? Baby Viebert had recognized him. No one forgets the person who first makes you eat the leaves of the pepper bush.

Norman thought of the hourglass of time that had funnelled him towards Baby Viebert, and the empty years fanning out ahead of him, away from her. Ignoring the illuminated seatbelt sign, he began his search in the sky at once, stumbling over the folk slumbering under their fleecy shrouds, pushing past their sleeping knees; he would seek her forever now. Headlong he rushed in his aeroplane through the freezing dark air, pulled onwards by the bright thread of the Pacific dawn. Surely fate could not be so easily evaded? Norman had only to live long enough to reach the second date. Surely there was one? Surely.

Neither Up Nor Down

THE WIND BLEW the palm fronds upwards and turned them into giant combs raking the mist. Penelope's hair stuck to her forehead. She clutched at her shoulder bag while the water braided and swirled around her thighs. A walk along a Tahitian beach in search of a sea cave was one thing, but wading through the streams that poured off the land into the ocean was enough to challenge even the strongest determination to be a good sport. Close by, chestnut-coloured hermit crabs crept in and out of the piles of coconut shells banked up against the trees.

"Em. Dickinson appreciated Melville's novels," said Charles. "Lots of coconuts and breadfruit in *Typee*. Em. made a mean gingerbread. Maybe she liked coconuts too."

"Did they cook much with coconut in the nineteenth century?"

"No idea." Charles was off again. He hated a question that he could not answer. Back behind the palms, a pointed peak rose up with shrubs growing out of it at right angles. White birds fluttered in front of the greenery like handkerchiefs dropped from a great height. Penelope wanted to pull herself up the peak, clinging onto the stubby trees until, triumphant and alone, she could stand looking out at the wide grey Pacific.

"And when they were up they were up, and when they were down they were down, and when they were only half-way up they were neither up nor down," she chanted.

"What?"

"Doesn't matter," said Penelope. Nothing she thought mattered. Thirty-five years ago they had been newly-weds touring Ireland with a rug and a volume of Yeats in the back seat of the car. Now, he was an irritating know-it-all, and she, she was a pudding.

Of course what Penelope thought did matter. Her former supervisor in food science, Howard McMurray, a mild man in a homespun sweater, had believed that Penelope's research was of key importance to fried chicken manufacturers everywhere. He had complimented her on her careful approach. Penelope had met Charles at Howard McMurray's annual Snowflake Do. Penelope had been charmed by the young professor with his careful way of dressing and his whimsical habit of embroidering the view with a sparkling quotation. Can you fall in love with a purple smoking jacket and a signet ring? Penelope had.

After his fourth gin and tonic Charles had pulled down some snowflake tinsel and draped it around Penelope's neck, stroking her hair. After his fifth gin and tonic he leaned heavily against the door frame and revealed that as a little boy he liked to balance on one foot. He had been practising this very skill when his sisters came to tell him that their mother had hanged herself in the pear tree at the bottom of the garden.

For many years he believed that if he could succeed in standing on one foot for a day and night, his mother might come back. As it happened, she had not died, but she had lingered, and that was worse. Charles did not like shadows in trees; he did not like to be alone. If Penelope did not already love him, she told herself that with time, she would. Upon finishing his sixth gin and tonic, Charles became rather ill, and Penelope took him home to her bed.

After their wedding, Penelope had concentrated on being a faculty wife because she imagined it was what she ought to do. In retrospect, her life had been governed by the sign of *ought:* I *ought* to be a better, thinner cook; I *ought* to have had more children; I *ought* to have found a job teaching adolescent girls how to roast chickens. Every Christmas she made plates of sugar cookies for Charles to take to the department party, she dropped off his late library books and searched for lost coffee mugs in his study. She had raised their son, a bookish child called Colin who had recently been granted tenure in the English department at Rook University. Colin claimed to be misunderstood, but in fact she knew him very well. He was a good boy, but in danger of becoming like his father. And what else did she do? When it came down to it she couldn't think what she had been doing.

In the meantime, Charles turned the way they met into a dinner-party joke. *It was her supervisor in food science who introduced us. You're studying the Browning Reaction? I said. Yes, she said, you know, to heat. Oh, I said, Brownings in Italy. No, she said, browning in turkeys.* She could see Charles now, snorting at his joke, tugging at his turtleneck. She should have stopped right there, at the Snowflake Do. But she had gone on with it, and the path had led here, to Tahiti, and this groping along the beach, looking for a sea cave where a long-dead writer might have had a rendezvous with a woman not his wife.

Soon they arrived at the edge of a garden where the trunk and limbs of a vast tree stretched along the ground like some great animal at leisure. Nailed to the tree was a sign in Tahitian. *Tabu,* the sign said, *keep out,* but not just in a *trespassers will be prosecuted* kind of a way. It was more sacred than that. *Tabu* was *keep out or something will get you.* Around about, thick banks of water fuchsia flourished unchecked in the humid air, the dark pattern of their leaves studded with scarlet flowers. Black crabs picked through the remnants of a balloon fish stuck on a fence post to dry, sidling sideways through a cloud of gnats. Penelope called ahead to Charles.

"I don't think we should go any further." She pointed at the post. "These crabs give me the creeps."

"Do you like this garden, is it yours?" asked Charles.

"What?" she said.

"Lowry, *Under the Volcano.*"

"Oh, that. This looks like private property."

"You're a bit scared, aren't you?" Charles tipped his hat back on his head. "Mistah Kurtz, he dead," he said.

"Don't mock me Charles."

"Miss-tah Kurtz," Charles said with more sibilance. Penelope turned her back.

"I heard you the first time," she said.

110

"Where are you going, Penn? Look, we've passed the peak and here's the end of the cove. This has to be the place that Stevenson refers to in the poem. The cave must be just around the corner."

"Charles, we have a plane to catch."

"Come on Penny, be a sport."

"I'll wait here for you."

Penelope sat in the green gloom swiping at mosquitoes. Once they might have walked to Stevenson's sea cave together. She would have laughed at Charles's obvious discomfort at having his trousers rolled up, he would have quoted somebody, and she would have thrown a piece of seaweed at him or threatened him with a crab. Now Penelope was glad that she would never find the sea cave, so that she would not have to hear the quotation with which Charles would adorn the view. Charles's mouth was a sea cave, with words rushing in and out of it, flecked with foam.

Charles hit the steering wheel with the flat of his hand, gleeful and shouting over the diesel engine.

"Magnificent, it was magnificent," he cried. "There's a hole in the cave roof, fringed with ferns. It's a natural pantheon. I stood there and recited the whole poem. The words just boomed and rolled about. I'm more convinced than ever. No one in the world knows that Stevenson ever came here, except the two of us. Certainly not his precious Fanny. Hah!"

Penelope sat silently, submitting to the roar. Poor Fanny. She was tired and she wanted to get on the plane.

"Let's see if there's anywhere to cut across," said Charles.

They drove up into a new subdivision where the houses sat on red earth blocks gouged out of the mountainside. One big rainfall and the houses could just slip off the side. Charles drove on the newly paved road with delight in his eyes. It was the look of being first. He had been first with Penelope too. Penelope had always assumed that she should comport herself as a married woman, a phrase that she always thought of in her grandmother's voice. She looked demurely, or sideways, under her eyelids at men. Charles's total freedom in this respect baffled her. When Charles was not reading he was talking about what he read with his female graduate students. And he would tell her about them too.

"Bit of a crush on that one," he would say in a false and hearty voice, but she never knew why she had to be told that at all.

After the houses ran out the road became steeper. A barrier prevented them from going any further. Charles pulled out around it and kept driving.

"Are you sure we can take this road?" asked Penelope.

"Of course, it's a brand new subdivision," said Charles.

"I don't think this is a good idea, Charles. Look at the creepers."

They had arrived at a tight corner with a space to pull over at the side. Tiny heart-shaped leaves on runners stretched out over the tarmac like lines of liquid spilling out from an unseen source. Charles sighed and pulled over.

"Alright, you win, Penny. Perhaps it would be an idea to go and see what's round the corner."

He disappeared around the edge of the cliff and Penelope was left alone with the gush of water in the bank beside her. The engine ticked as it cooled. The urge to drive away tugged at her like the currents pouring off the land into the sea. She saw the road empty, and Charles returning to find nothing but creepers fanning out over the centre line. Penelope climbed over into the driver's seat. Her shorts caught on the gear stick and ripped. She started the car.

At the airport, Penelope returned the rental car and lumbered along with both of their bags in a trolley. She found a seat between a pillar and a bank of tropical plants. After an hour had passed she thought, he knows now, he knows that I have gone. She thought of the puffer fish on the post and its empty eye sockets. *I have snapped,* she thought. *Like a sugar snap pea. I have no idea what I am doing.* The young couple next to her moved off to resume their kissing beside the bank machine. Several leis were draped around the girl's neck and her boyfriend rested his big hands on her shoulders, leaving brown creases in the waxy flowers. Once she had been kissed like that, with intent, on a hot hillside in Ireland, while the wind flicked through the pages of Yeats, discarded along with the empty wine bottle. Penelope had left her own lei in the hotel refrigerator.

"Penelope Pilchard, it's Penelope isn't it?"

She lifted her head out of her hands. Two puffy faces floated into her field of vision. It was Bevan and May Calder from Brockville in their matching sweatsuits.

"Penelope, dear," said May, "fancy finding you here. But where's Charles?"

They looked around, as if he might be hiding behind the tropical plants. Bevan and May's cultivated innocence belied their thirst for gossip. They pecked about like hens in the dust, looking for titbits of news to relay to their travel club and their Bible-study group.

"He's dealing with the rental car. You know what it's like," said Penelope. Bevan and May did indeed know. They launched into a story about sitting in the plane near some man who later pushed his wife down a crevasse.

"Can you imagine that?" said May. "We saw it on the news. And I said to Bevan that's the glacier man isn't it? And on the plane he accused Bevan of taking his pillow."

"He was an impolite what-have-you, if you'll pardon my French, Penelope," said Bevan.

May nodded. "I said to Bevan he ought to tell the police what he knew, about the pillow."

"Well they got him, didn't they?" said Bevan, "and that's the main thing. Time to move on through, love. Wouldn't want to miss the flight. Are you on this one Penelope or later?"

"Three AM," Penelope replied.

"You've got a long time to wait." May pursed her lips and made a sucking noise in the air beside Penelope's cheek. "Tell Charles that we said hello."

Watching the matching bottoms of Bevan and May recede into the crowd, Penelope realized that she was no better than their glacier man. Her actions were not private, they belonged in the tabloids and the Calders would make sure of it. If she were going to leave Charles, she had to leave him somewhere altogether more ordinary, on the way to having her hair done or in the vegetable aisle at the supermarket. In the meantime she ought to find him and make a renewed effort to bring him back into her, into their life. He could not live forever in the literary room next door.

It was well after midnight by the time her taxi arrived at the barrier at the top of the deserted road.

"My husband, là-bas," said Penelope, pointing, trying to make the driver understand where she wanted to go to. "Mon mari," and finally, "mon amour est là." But the driver refused to go beyond the barrier, so she asked him to wait before she got out of the car.

Darkness covered the cliffs. The moon had risen and transformed the sky over the sea into a luminous upturned bowl. Penelope's stomach retracted in fear that Charles might have been murdered, that crabs could even now be picking over his eyes. Surely he would be there, sitting on a log in the half-light, crossing and re-crossing his legs, twirling his hat around on his clenched fist, reading the *Times Literary Supplement* that he kept in his pocket, or stroking his beard into a sharp point. Penelope recalled the things he had once said to her, that she was the good solid earth beneath his feet, the sky over his head, the sun that kept the shadows under the leaves at bay. She thought of the way his mouth curled up at the edges, so that it looked like he was smiling when he was not. She hurried and her sandals went clack-clack upon the road.

Charles was smaller than she remembered. He stood up as she approached.

"There you are," he said, as if she were a sock that he had mislaid under the bed. "May I inquire just what you thought you were doing, taking off like that?"

"I'm sorry. I needed to be by myself."

"I see," said Charles. There was a tight look about his mouth.

Penelope saw her husband's face framed by the great Pacific Ocean that glistened and stretched to the moon. They were trapped on this island, with no hope of swimming away. A truce had to be reached before they could travel on together.

"I'm glad you're still here," she said. "I thought you might have gone to find a *glimmering girl.*"

"I am not in the mood for funny phrases," said Charles. "I have been waiting for you for three hours. Can you imagine how that makes me feel? Obviously not. Now. Shall we catch our plane before it's too late?"

They stayed far apart as they walked up the hill. In the taxi, Charles leaned back and pretended to sleep.

"Please don't do that again, Penny," he said, his eyes still shut.

Penelope was silent.

"Ever."

But Penelope had nothing to say. She was terribly afraid that she would do it again. They were in the middle of nowhere. All around the island the ocean glittered and beckoned. She sought out his hand and held it in the dark chirruping night.

Through the Gates

A T FIRST SIGHT, there was nothing special about St. James's Church. A stubby square tower sat up like thumb at one end, and at the other, a broad curve of windows overlooked a gully full of tree ferns. Inside, the couple lay collapsed beside the altar like tramps, their heads propped up on the stucco wall, straining to catch a glimpse out the window at some marvel in the sky. Eventually the woman sat up and rubbed the back of her head.

"I give up Gord, it's no use. You can't see the glacier from in here any more. Maybe twenty years ago. I told you we'd have to drive up close in the car." Rita used the corner of the altar to pull herself up off the floor. She pulled down her jersey, puffed up her hair out of habit.

"Maybe if I get down a bit lower," said Gordon.

"You can't go lower Gord, you're on the floor. It's no good. Here, take my hand and let's be going."

Really it wasn't their habit to drop into churches in this way, but since Amanda had phoned from Canada with the news, Rita had taken to going into churches of all kinds. Private gods, public Gods, ancient gods, invented gods; she called on them all to spare her daughter. Gord, on the other

117

hand, kept his spiritual side tucked away out of sight, like his bald spot, which he hid under a flat brown cap, with a few grey curls licking out the back of it. Pressed, he would call himself a bet hedger in the God department. Still, he always tagged along when Rita went into churches.

Actually Rita and Gord were lucky that the church was open at all. A good fifty years had passed since the church had been built, with its view of the Franz Josef glacier out the front windows, designed to prompt prayer among the tree ferns and praise for the high and icy work of the Almighty. Now it was 1986 and the volume of tourists in the area was already increasing along with the number of fish-and-chip dinners served at The BellBird's Table, the theft of car radios and motel visiting books, and even the brass candlesticks from the very church that they had been lying down in.

Gordon was disappointed that he could not see the glacier. A great uncle had brought him to this church once before as a young lad. He remembered the twisted fingers of the uncle, gently pushing him to kneel down and crane his neck to see its great gritty tongue. He'd always liked the idea of the inevitable flow of ice that crushed mountains as it moved. Since Amanda's phone call, the glacier seemed to have taken up residence inside his skull, scraping along like a great cold headache. He wondered whether the man existed who would be patient enough to lie down and be run over by a glacier. It would be a slow death. A decade would be long enough, surely. After that the glacier would bear you along towards the sea, with a creaking, crackling pebble-strewn slowness; a good and natural way to go.

Throughout their West Coast road trip, Gord was continuously reminded of standard six and Mr. Watson in front of the blackboard, rapping with a ruler at the words *Plato's cave.* Something about light and shadow flickering on the wall, but you had to go outside the cave for the real thing. Once, when Amanda had been seven and leaping about in the shallows at Waikouaiti beach, the slanting green fronds of the aurora australis had processed in stately fashion over the clouds above her. Gord had thought to himself, *shadows and archetypes; gifts from beyond,* but he had explained it to Amanda in terms of charged particles because even then he could not remember enough about the cave.

Rita stepped into a shaft of light, holding a brochure that she had pulled out of a rack beside the church door. She had left her glasses in the car and now she held the brochure at arm's length.

"The brochure says that Hinehukatere was climbing in the mountains with her boyfriend Tawe, and he fell, and she wept," she said.

"And her tears made the glacier?" Gord came up beside her. "That's a lot of crying."

"Hinehukatere is called the Avalanche Girl," said Rita. "Do you think Amanda has a boyfriend?"

Gordon shrugged and turned the corners of his mouth down.

"Is that how you catch it?" he asked.

The break away had been planned well before the phone call, and Amanda had insisted that she felt fine, and that it would be weeks before she knew the results of the next set of tests. In any case, Rita said that she couldn't possibly wait by the phone that long so they set out inland from Christchurch, as arranged, and passed across the great divide to the wild West Coast. When they got to the coastal highway they turned left and headed south, and that was where Gordon began seeing what he thought of as archetypal forms, because the rainfall made everything so much bigger there. First they drove past a great matai tree beside the road, huge and towering with a trunk as spacious as a spare room. Gord could only see twenty feet up into the tree before the thicket of branches blocked his view, but even then he could see the flax and ferns and moss that sprouted along its branches. He thought of the great upsuck of sap and the endless supporting of life among the branches for a thousand years. He took off his cap and rubbed his head. *Feeble, that's what humans are,* he thought, *feeble by comparison.*

From the beginning, Amanda had been a bright child, filled with a kind of light that manifested itself as an intense curiosity. She crouched in the back garden over a rock that she had just overturned, peeling off the slugs and watching the colonists underneath scatter into the dense growth of the pale grassroots. After her undergraduate degree, she went to study micro-organisms in Ontario, working on an MSc that stretched into a long PhD and on into a postdoc. As long as she could get funding, she could go on lifting up rocks and observing what was underneath them, at least that's how Rita thought of it. Gord and Rita had visited Amanda at Rook

University once, but they had been so cold in the tiny apartment where the ice feathered the windows like expensive crystal. Outside the snow creaked underfoot and the wind bit into their faces with a nastiness that surprised them. Not once did they find a real cup of tea. The waitress insisted on giving them a glass of hot water with the teabag still in its packet on the plate underneath. Explaining made no difference. North America was not for them.

Gord drove for a while and Rita looked out the window, watching the sky and the glacier and the tree ferns and the crashing surf. She was surprised that her eyes were wide enough apart to take in the view, but there it was, the whole water cycle from the beginning to the end and back around again, all framed by the windscreen.

Rita had behind her a lifetime of putting spare change in the social money box labelled good deeds, pouring out tea for elderly folk, standing on street corners in a cold spring breeze to sell poppies for the Returned Services Association, but when she came to think about death, she could only sense a kind of tumbling inside a great cosmic washing machine full of atoms and liquids being poured in and drained out. *The amount of energy in the world is constant.* That much she recalled from science at St. Ethelred's School where lab-coated Miss Scott performed dangerous acts with minute amounts of sodium that in the off-hours lurked under oil on the storeroom shelf, curious as an artichoke heart or an embryo. Miss Scott made manifest the possibility of a bright twinkling light under the right circumstances and a certain diminishment of the material world as a result. With the self, as opposed to Miss Scott's twitchy experiments on Wednesdays at 11, one never knew when.

The next morning Gord and Rita walked around the edge of Lake Matheson. They went early, as the guide book suggested, along a lakeside boardwalk covered in chicken wire. Eventually they came onto a small railed jetty that gave them a view, *the* view of the mountain. Before them Mt. Cook/Aoraki, with a spike and a rip in the sound of its name, slashed up through the blue canvas of the air. How many years had Rita looked at the same image on the back of her bridge cards? Here it was, in the flesh, in the stone. And without the implacable force of the peak ripping into the sky, there could be no famous image on the backs of playing cards, no comfort in bridge, no quiet discussions among women.

The peak's reflection rippled as a duck tracked a vee across the surface of the water. Rita did not know if there was a cure for whatever Amanda had. She did not know if you could only catch the disease in North America or if you could catch it in New Zealand too. She thought about the Avalanche Girl, and the torrent of frozen tears running from the sky to the sea. A cold river of grief was to coming to sweep her and all her life before it.

She sat down with a thump on the jetty. Gord came up and stood over her, rolling up his jersey into a lumpy pillow.

"You all right? You're looking pale. You might want this. It's damp."

"If anything ever happens to me Gord, you'll find me here."

"Nothing's going to happen, Rita. We'll manage. Do you need a tissue?"

"No thanks, dear. I just came over a bit wobbly that's all." She stood up, leaving an imprint on the dewy boards, taking the arm he offered and leaning into his body.

"Come on, let's go back to the car, love," said Gord. "I think there's still some tea in the thermos."

They idled down the coast through the afternoon. The sun heated up the inside of the car. Just beyond Whataroa a sign invited them to visit a colony of white herons. Gord slowed the car before the turnoff.

"Shall we?"

Rita shook her head. All those big white birds flying up from the trees and settling again. She had seen them in a documentary, with their feathers spread out like finger bones in the sun.

"I don't think I can, Gord. I feel like it's all speaking. We must go home, in case there's news."

"I know, Rita," he said.

"You do, you really do?" Rita frowned.

"We must try, you know, Rita," he said. "The problem is that we don't know very much about it. There must be a pamphlet."

"I just feel so helpless." Rita shook her head again.

"Cheese sandwich at the Haast café?"

"Yes. Then home."

The Land Below

THE LAST TWO PARTIES of the day saw no adult albatrosses at all, so it was up to Rae to make sure that the visitors did not go away disappointed. She tried to create the missing birds, making huge gestures with her arms in front of the audiovisual display, dramatising facts about the dangers posed by drift-net fishing, and the sly thieving nature of stoats, but nothing compared with a glimpse of a white wing sweeping around the headland where the Otago harbour meets the South Pacific. You couldn't conjure it: it was, or it was not. Well, at least the tourists got plenty of pictures of the two fat chicks on the windy hillside, wisps of down fluttering at the back of their necks.

Just after five o'clock she hung up her vest and took her handbag out of her locker.

"Well that's it then. I'll see you on Monday, Sheila."

Sheila looked up from the statistics on her screen.

"You okay, Rae?"

"Yes, thanks, just a bit tired I suppose."

Rae brushed the back of her hand across her eyes. She was glad that Sheila had come to work at the albatross colony. A constant kind of friendship had grown up between them, based on having been at school together. To know someone at thirteen is really to know them. She remembered the greeting they had shared on Sheila's first day, as if it had not been thirty years, but just a long summer holiday since they had seen each other. Rae walked across the car park and down to the railing at the cliff's edge. A gull in red stockings ran before her, skirting the puddles full of pink sky. Below her the cliff fell away in a cascade of fleshy ice plant starred with orange flowers. When she looked back she saw Sheila waving as if she had something to tell her. Rae walked back up to the building.

"Rae, I was wondering if you'd like to go to Sandfly Bay tomorrow afternoon, to watch the penguins come in?"

"I thought you usually worked on Saturdays?" Rae searched her pockets for her car keys.

"Not this Saturday. Interested?"

"What time?"

"About three?"

"Sounds good."

The two women hugged. Rae could not remember how they had fallen into this hugging. It had started as a New Year thing, but each time they held on a fraction longer. It was only a matter of time before they would look each other in the eye afterwards and one of them would push away a loose strand of hair from the other's face.

As Rae swung in and out of the bays along the harbour road back to Dunedin, the sun crept up the hills behind the city. The street lights had come on by the time she turned into the driveway of the villa on the crown of the hill. She locked the car. The air was sharp on the lungs and hazy with smoke from the wood fires down in the valley.

On the floor inside the front door lay a familiar packet addressed to her mother, postmarked from France. Rae picked it up and threw it onto the kitchen table without looking at it. She knew what it contained: Gauloises, the annual reminder of the year that her mother had spent at the Sorbonne before marriage claimed her.

Rae took down her mother's apron from the hook beside the stove, found matches and relit the pilot light. In the days when everyone was switching to electric ovens, her mother had insisted that gas gave better heat. I'll make Dad some scones, she thought, thinking of her mother's floured hands turning and tossing the dough as if she were slapping laundry on a rock, then throwing the trays into the oven through a crack in the door as if a volcano might billow out into the room. There was nothing her father liked better than scones and raspberry jam. Making jam had been one of the last things her mother had done before they left to spend New Year's Day with the Leamings. Just after a quick stop for tea at Catcher's Hotel, while the Leamings waited to greet them with leftover Christmas pudding and honey-glazed ham, Rae's father lost feeling in his left side and slumped forward over the wheel. The car veered across the road into a power pole.

It was always surprising how few pots of jam came out of a batch. All that washing and picking through, taking out the mouldy and the squashed, and they boil away to nothing. Rae found a jar at the back of the cupboard and tapped on it. The cellophane seal was concave and tight as a skin.

While the scones cooked she turned over the package on the table, looking at the French stamps. Rae knew so little about her mother's life before her marriage, especially the mythical year when she studied at the Sorbonne, boiling eggs in a kettle and sleeping in a hat, scarf and black mittens. Each year the French flatmate, who must now be heading for seventy, sent a packet of Gauloises to New Zealand. The cigarettes would arrive squashed, battered and stale, yet without fail Rae's mother would retreat to the bottom of the garden where she would smoke one or two each afternoon for a week. Rae and her father raked the leaves into piles around the unseeing woman wreathed in smoke.

Rae went about the house picking up bits and pieces that might help her father to pass another moment in the nursing home where the floor polisher hummed night and day in the corridor. She found a newspaper cutting about the retiring dean of the medical school, and an article about a giant squid found floating on the surface of the sea.

The physiotherapist was in the room when Rae arrived, putting away the mirror that she had been using to encourage Rae's father's left side to move. While Rae watched, her father succeeded in twitching his thumb a fraction.

Rae's father was a retired medical man. He enjoyed his golf, and he enjoyed sitting in front of the television diagnosing the weather lady's goitre problem. There were no mysteries for Rae's father. The body was a machine, a bundle of processes, and like a car, it could be fixed. Rae's mother, on the other hand, had been a machine that could not be fixed. *I'm sorry Ms. Small, there is nothing we can do.* Nothing we can do. There's always something you can do. There were always scones to make, shirts to iron.

Dr. Small chewed laboriously at a scone, pronouncing it delicious. There were crumbs and a coffee stain on his jumper. They talked about the coming election, about snow in the forecast.

"If only I could get out of this darned chair," he said. "You will look after the house after I'm gone, won't you? Don't let them change anything."

"Oh Dad, you mustn't talk like that."

"Well I'm not going to last forever, but your mother wouldn't like it if they changed things around." Rae thought of the mottled red carpet and the gas heater with the plastic logs and the revolving bulb that flickered inside them. There was everything to change. It was a young couple's renovating dream.

"Don't worry," she said.

"Forget what I said about staying in the house, Rae. Sell it. You have your own life to live."

An old hot vein of frustration opened up in Rae. She took a deep breath.

"It's alright Dad. Don't worry," she said.

On Saturday afternoon Rae and Sheila met in a farmer's field high up above the Pacific. A sharp wind blew the macrocarpa trees further into their ancient stunted shapes. Signs pointed visitors over the paddock towards the giant sand hill at the entrance to the beach, warning them not to bother the lambs. Rae took off her boots and rolled up her jeans. The two women picked their way down the sand hill, eyes narrowed against the wind, both remembering their thirteen-year-old selves on a school outing, launching themselves off the top of the hill with whoops and bounds. The sand hill seemed smaller now, trodden down. At the bottom the wind-blown sand stung their ankles and hissed in the tussock. The beach was empty, except for a sandy piece of driftwood that developed flippers and a pointed nose, and lumbered off into the dunes. Sand had banked up against the sea side of the bird hide and they both had to work to get the door open.

"My feet are so cold, I think I'm going to die!" Rae pulled her socks out of her pocket and used them to rub at her heels. "I don't know why I took my boots off in the first place," she said.

"Old reflex, I suppose," said Sheila. She opened the shutters, letting in a thin sliver of shoreline and the winter sky. "I haven't been here for years."

"Me neither," said Rae.

Rae sat on a bench in front of the window, and Sheila turned and lifted each of Rae's feet in turn. She brushed the sand off matter-of-factly as if it were not Rae's foot at all, but a piece of driftwood that she had picked up to take home.

"Better?" asked Sheila.

"Yes, thanks," said Rae.

A penguin paddled in the waves just offshore, craning its neck to see whether the coast was clear. Soon another joined it, and soon there were three. When they felt safe they reared up off their chests like little toys and waddled towards the shelter of the flax bushes, inching their way up the hillside on their private tracks. The women sat side by side on the narrow bench, no longer touching, not Rae, not Sheila at all, just two women who had driven out to watch the penguins come in.

I wonder how long I can carry on not being me? Rae thought. *This isn't me. Or perhaps it is me, but not a me that I know yet. I must see if Dad's nails need clipping.* She tucked the thought away, the same way her mother used to come in from the garden tucking stray wisps of hair behind her ears.

Rae could feel Sheila's palm warm against her ear, silencing the sea, leaving only the sound of her blood.

"You should look after yourself, you're looking a bit thin," said Sheila. Rae was silent. "You okay Rae?"

"I don't know about this," said Rae.

"What's there to know?" asked Sheila.

What was there to know? Only the agapanthus and the empty clothesline.

"Rae, come and stay with me for a while. Let me look after you for a bit. No, that's not what I mean. Come and live with me Rae, we'd be good together."

It was as easy as that. *We'd be good together.*

"Thanks, Sheila." Rae looked at Sheila's small, perfect earlobe, unable to look her in the eye. "I'll think about it, I really will."

131

"Do," said Sheila, placing a hand on each of Rae's shoulders. "Promise me you will." She kissed her on the cheek.

They left the bird hide and walked back towards the car. They passed only one family coming the other way, two adults and a child who ran in and out of the sea, oblivious to the cold waves.

"You don't have to go home, Rae. Come to my place."

"Thanks, I know I don't, but I always go up to see Dad about this time."

"I'll see you on Monday then?"

"Yes, I'm in from 11 until 4."

The numbers defined the space between them. Of course Rae would see Sheila. There was work to do. If a life together were to be arranged, it would be thought out with the practicality of grown women, of egg sandwiches and a thermos of hot water, of teabags in a separate container. It could wait until Monday. They got into their cars. It was a relief not to be buffeted by the wind any more. Rae drove home past the spiked silhouette of a cabbage tree against golden sky, and a lone sheep, watching.

Rae went up the path to her parents' house, past the hydrangeas with their wet mottled leaves. *I don't know how to proceed at all from here,* she thought, *and I should. I am a middle-aged woman.*

It was getting late. She picked up the package from the kitchen table. The postmark said Toulouse. She found scissors and carefully slit the brown paper apart. Inside was a packet of cigarettes, unsealed and then resealed. She pulled the cigarettes out. There was no note, but on each cigarette a single French word was printed: plain, domestic words that ordered and reordered, told a different tale each time. *Monday, coffee, bed, chair, cheese, blanket, Wednesday, bread, Burgundy, Thursday, grass, cemetery.* One cigarette had initials on it, her mother's maiden name, K.M. Rae thought of her mother smoking random dreams at the bottom of the garden. Over time the famous year in France had fragmented into single words, brittle as shreds of old tobacco. She looked at a cigarette that said L.F. de R. for a long time before she put it in her pocket.

It was getting late. Rae ran a bath and got into it before the enamel had finished warming up. She lay there until the water was nearly cold, occasionally flapping her hands over the surface of the water. She thought of Sheila in her waxed jacket doing battle against the wind, the wind lifting her curling hair away from her forehead, her profile dark and intent.

Women do it all the time, pack up, leave, move in with their pastoral care officers, their nutritionists, physiotherapists, local health-food co-op owners; women who touch their skins and minister to their bodies and minds. Daily, thousands of women arrive with squashy bags full of sweatshirts at the front door of a place that isn't yet home. There was nothing to it. But how could she do that, if she did not really know what she felt? Why was it so hard to feel anything at all?

She dried herself and dressed and went out to find a few things in the garden to take up to her father. Rae's mother had loved flowers, but not in an ordered way. The garden was filled with masses of nodding aguilegia seeded in clumps. The dried sticks of the flower heads stood above the scarred and dying leaves. Rae clipped some late heartsease and looked at their inquiring faces, wondering what her mother would have said about her father being in a home, and what she would have said about Sheila.

Rae's father had been at medical school with Sheila's father, so it was assumed that the two girls would get along. At school Sheila had been an aggressive hockey player, often getting called out for having her stick raised too high. She was at her best at school camps, making bivouacs and jumping into cold rivers with her clothes on. In class she fought with her teachers, struggled against their facts and their requirements, and their sheer stupidity. Her burning anger with the world gave her a kind of power. Many of the girls felt it and avoided her.

Not long after Sheila started school, Rae's parents invited Sheila and her father to lunch. Sheila had been patently bored. When the adult talk turned from fire alarms to stomach cancer, the girls asked to be excused. They went outside, following the path into the orchard. The quince leaves hung motionless in the warm autumn air, and walnuts in their twisted black cloaks lay ready to be picked up off the ground before the rats that lived in the hedge could get at them.

One of Rae's chores was to gather up the cooking apples and put them in a basket in the corner of the kitchen. On Friday nights, Rae's mother would sit behind the scales, slicing the apples with a firm hand. Rae had not collected apples for days and a strong wind had scattered them on the ground. Sheila picked up an apple and threw it against the garage wall. The apple hit the bricks with a satisfying thunk, split in two and dropped off, leaving behind a few fragments. She picked up another and another, smashing the apples against the brick wall with fierce joy. *Sheila is happy,* thought Rae. *Sheila is having a good time at my house.* She felt proud to be pleasing Sheila when no one else could, so she stood and watched while Sheila went about gathering all the apples from the orchard and even pulling some off the trees and throwing them against the wall.

On Sunday afternoon Rae's mother was raking leaves for a bonfire. The smoke lay curled about the trees.

"Will you look at what those boys have done to my apples? It's a crying shame. All my apples." She pointed at the bruised and smashed fruit lying under the garage wall, the brown fragments clinging to the bricks.

"That's terrible," said Rae. She went inside to learn her French verbs. For a while after the apple incident, Rae avoided Sheila in the school corridor.

Rae sat in the chair on the porch and looked out at the grey lines of the sea. On Monday she would make her lame excuses to Sheila, and their friendship and everything else would be broken. All she could think of was the sadness in her mother's voice as she looked at the smashed apples. And in the same voice she could hear her mother asking, *where is love in all this?* Except that her mother had never said anything of the sort.

That afternoon she found her father in a sombre mood.

"It was my fault Rae. I killed her," he said.

"Dad, you had a stroke. There was nothing you could do."

Rae's mother had died shortly after her arrival at the hospital. It was a blessing, everyone had said so.

"Dad, I'm thinking of going away for a break. Just a fortnight. Will you be all right without me? My friend Sheila says she will look in on you. You remember Sheila's father Rex Haworth from medical school?"

"Fine physician."

Rae had no idea whether Sheila would agree to it.

"So where are you going off to Rae?"

"Mum's cigarettes arrived the other day, and I thought I might go to France." She tried to make it sound as casual as going to the beach.

"That's a long way from here. What do you want in France dear?"

"I want to tell that French woman about mother."

"Who?"

"You know, the cigarette friend, the flatmate from the Sorbonne."

"Well you're not going to find her, dear," he said.

"Why not?"

"Because it wasn't a woman."

"It wasn't a woman?"

"No. I think you'll find it was a chap." With difficulty Rae's father turned his head and looked out the window.

"Oh," said Rae.

She turned and looked with him out at the wet

rhododendrons. Raindrops were making their way down the pane, separating and colliding and separating again. So change was possible, even after death. Deep inside Rae a great bird lifted off and the land below fell away. She was high above the white caps and there was no sound but the wind.

"Will you be all right Dad?"

"Yes. No. I don't know. You go on. I'll still be here."

"Dad, are you sure?"

"I suppose so. Does this Sheila friend of yours make scones?"

"I'll ask Dad, I'll ask."

Neptune's Necklace

THE TRACK TO THE salt marsh was crowded with lupins poised to shed their seeds with a twisted cracking of each blackened pod. Once on the sand, Hattie let Shelley off his leash and set out towards the channel at the harbour entrance. Shelley ran ahead, tongue out, weaving in and out of the tide lines as he sniffed the morning news. There had been a storm in the night. Papery sea lettuce and the green nubbled beads of Neptune's necklace lay slung about the flats in greater quantities than usual. More rain would come around eleven o'clock, and more again in the afternoon. Around five it might clear up. It was always this way.

When Hattie reached the end of the flats, she turned to walk parallel with the channel towards the sea. There she sensed the usual clutch of child-sized shades running before her along the beach, shouting at each other to come and look at a dead mollymawk where it had washed up against a piece of driftwood. Obediently she also stopped to look at the tide-rinsed bird, noting the sand already banked up against the sharp curve of its useless beak. Hattie felt the presence of the long-dead children every morning, and every morning she had to stop and wait until the children's cries faded and her heart rate slowed. She turned towards the sea, and, frowning, concentrated on a couple of discombobulated sea slugs lolling like turds in the tide. Further along, bouquets of sea tulips lay tossed up among the confetti of shells. She passed them by; she had painted the fleshy heads sagging on their goose necks often enough.

Nearby, in the depths of the channel grew an entire field of sea tulips, endlessly flowering and feeding in the sea currents. Funny things, sea tulips. They start off as animals and end up as plants. Hattie often imagined the pattern that the stems and heads might make en masse, waving in the depths of the channel. She had a weakness for pattern and she knew it; wherever three or more objects appeared together, well, that created significance, even if it was accidental. Sometimes she would deny herself pattern; deny the repetitions that created rhythm and the links that made narrative. She would try to paint the object as itself alone and not seen in relation to any other thing, except her own eyes. Other times she fell off the wagon entirely and silk-screened whole rolls of wallpaper just to get the patterns out of her system. Some days she did nothing but sip her cognac by the fire.

Hattie. Her real name was Heliotrope. Her mother had been an artist's model back when there were only two models in the whole city of Dunedin and all decent New Zealanders considered modelling to be tantamount to prostitution. Heliotrope. What a name for a child. It was preposterous, redolent of ragged satin undergarments strewn over an ancient odorous carpet. Hattie, on the other hand, was not a bad name for an artist, and Hattie had decided to be an artist at the age of six.

Now Hattie was seventy-three. She had yet to fall upon getting out of bed, and she had no children to worry about her. She had a good dog, a good stick, a seldom used lock on the door, and no external display of rot, barring the wrinkles and the rough patches. She had already decided to move into town once she could no longer make her morning walk, but she could not really see herself studying a hand of bridge in an overheated lounge decorated with the flesh-coloured spears of gladioli in vases.

The ghostly children scattered and disappeared. Ahead Hattie caught sight of the last three in a chain of linked dredge buckets, long since beached after the end of their useful life hauling silt out of the shipping channel. Occasionally, after a good storm, a section of the buckets would surface in bas-relief against the pale sand, hefty and mottled like the bellies of chained ogres or the vertebrae of long buried dinosaurs. Hattie loved the dredge buckets, mainly because she never knew when they would appear. For months she had wanted to paint a dredge bucket triptych. Now she stepped up to take a closer look at the spackled line of the sand around the edges of the hulks where they lay submerged in the sand.

She patted her pockets and cursed. No sketchbook. Irritated, she walked around the buckets, memorizing for later.

When she got back to the house Hattie quickly drew what she could remember of the dredge buckets. The most difficult thing was catching their weight in relation to the sand, which at one moment could lie waterlogged and banked up, and at another could blow away. By the time she had finished, the mid-morning clouds had rolled in from the sea and the rain had begun.

While she drank her coffee she looked out the window and considered the childish shades. Once a day she permitted herself to think about them, no more. Even once a day was too much, by some people's standards. The shades were girls, all of them, and one of the shades was Hattie's daughter, running ahead, the first to tumble shrieking and splashing into the waves. The other girls shouted for her to wait, while they scrambled over the dunes behind her. Far behind, two mothers ambled along the beach, towels slung about their necks, linked tennis shoes dangling from their wrists, slowed down with baskets of iced buns and fruit, spare sunhats, seaweed strands and shells. Hattie remembered that the mothers had been discussing varieties of cooking apple.

She poked at the fire. The grate was small and it never gave off a great deal of heat, but the colour always warmed her, as did the bronze velvet curtain that screened off her bedroom. Absently she looked out the window. At the time, she really had been very good friends with the mother of the other two girls. They had congratulated themselves on sharing the same values. Neither of them had any time for husbands or fathers. Painting, baking bread, sprouting mung beans in jars on windowsills, knitting chunky jumpers, and being ready to swoop in like hungry petrels to scoop their children out of difficulty;

this was what was important. In the end, they turned out to have nothing in common at all.

The rain had settled in for the afternoon, slanting along in front of the headland, striating the reddish rock and the green slopes on top with grey. Without seeing them she knew that the houses in the settlement looked like wet boulders lying close to the land.

Shelley was barking. A couple, a boy and a girl, students perhaps, were coming down the driveway. They were hurrying, holding a large rust-coloured jumper over their heads for shelter.

Hattie saw them pass the side of the house, heard the squelching of their sandshoes on the gravel. She held still while she waited for the knock at the door and wondered whether she would answer it. She moved into the kitchen and took a quick glance out the window at them. Young and lithe as eels, the couple stood on the step laughing in the wet air that was no discomfort, since they were together. The girl's dark hair stuck to her cheeks in licks and inverted question marks. The straps of a purple bra plainly showed around the edges of her robin's egg blue tank top. She wore a necklace of seaweed. Hattie decided to open the door for the sake of the necklace, if not for the colour of the shirt.

The girl spoke first.

"Sorry to bother you," she said, "but we were wondering if we could use your phone? We forgot ours. The mini won't start."

Hattie had owned a mini herself once. She still remembered with pleasure the cresting waves of mechanical sound between the gear changes and the flashing of the speckled tarmac in the road passing by through the holes in the floor.

"Of course. Do come in out of the rain." She held the door open for them. They wiped their sandy shoes on the mat and came into the galley kitchen, glancing around at the low slanted ceiling, taking in the cracked enamelled sink and the leaking tap. There was sand on the backs of their necks from where they had been lying in the sea grass before it began to rain.

The boy dropped the wet jumper on the floor by the door.

"I'll just leave these here." The girl had picked up a bunch of sea tulips attached to a mussel shell. She placed them on top of the wet jumper where the sandy heads lolled back like pale chunks of meat.

"This way to the telephone," said Hattie.

The students followed her up into the sitting room where the long windows on either side of the fireplace let in strips of light and a view of cabbage trees threshing the grey sky. The couple stood with their backs to the fire, rubbing their hands together and casting surreptitious glances around the room and into the studio beyond.

"It was only an eight-hundred-dollar car," the girl said, "I hope they don't have to tow us back into town. We were chased by a seal," she said happily.

"That would be Victor the sea lion. He does get territorial," said Hattie. She showed the boy where the phone was.

He dialled and spoke. His voice sounded impatient as well as apologetic. She could see that he was a good boy, even if he did not take particular care over the jumper that his mother had knitted for him.

"We'll be late for dinner," he said, turning to look at the girl.

"With his mother," said the girl, blushing. "Are you an artist? It's so wonderful to be in the house of a real artist. I'm studying art history. I have to do an essay on someone contemporary and maybe I could come back one day and talk to you about your work, and your influences?" The words came hurrying out, ending in a raised squeak.

"I'm usually working at this time of day," said Hattie. "I don't have any influences. But feel free to look around."

The girl blushed again. She stepped up into the studio where Hattie saw her taking in the shelf of maquettes, the notebooks recording the heights of the tides, the shells and the sea glass, the bones and the buoys, the driftwood and the comparative logs tracking the heights of the tides and the patterns of the seasons, all in the attempt to make sense of the anomaly that had overtaken the rhythm one summer afternoon.

"I'll make tea," she said.

She was annoyed to find her hands shaking as she filled the kettle. It bumped awkwardly against the tap as she filled it. The girl came back in. She seemed tall in the galley kitchen.

"I'm sorry if we have disturbed you. Is there anything I can do to help?" she asked.

"You can find the cups if you like," said Hattie. "I like your necklace," she added, trying to make up for not having any influences. Tied to a piece of twine, the fresh fan of nubbled sea beads lay at the girl's neck like a damp hand. "You did a good job of tying it together. My daughter always used fishing tackle to attach the ones she made me, but they do tend to come apart after they dry up."

"Thank you," said the girl, laughing. "Kevin made it for me. We are in love," she added shyly. "Gosh, I don't know what made me say that. Is that your daughter?" She pointed at a discoloured snapshot of a little girl waving a large piece of seaweed.

Hattie nodded.

"She was one of three," Hattie began, and she saw the girls smacking the water with the flat of their hands to make it spray up at each other, heard them shrieking. Over the years she had painted these children in so many different ways, descending among the sea tulips as water babies, naked except for fins, or bedecked in brassy oval leaves like weedy sea dragons. She had painted them as adolescent albatrosses that have left the cliffs, never to return to land. She had painted them as the girl guides they were, gifted at tying knots and at making cups of tea, but unable to solve the puzzle of the currents.

The sound of the rain on the tin roof slowed to a series of dull raps. The young man hurried in.

"They'll be coming soon. We should wait by the car," he said. The girl nodded.

She put down her barely sipped tea.

"She was one of three girls," Hattie finished. They were not listening. *We are in love,* the girl had said. Why not, for once, leave it at that?

Hattie stood watching them go. At the end of the driveway they stopped and glanced back at the house. She ought to have turned away by now. But she could not take her eyes off the girl, the same age as her granddaughter might have been, and the boy, who might have been her boyfriend, and the jumper, which she might have knitted for him. To that girl, I am nothing but a tissue of influences, she thought. She took off her glasses. The rusty jumper and the eggshell blue tank top stood out against the dusty darkness of the macrocarpa hedge and the strip of grass beside the road. I will paint them, she thought, as a tartan rug for picnics, and lying under it, a sea lion.

Hattie collected the cups and turned the tap onto the dishes in the sink. The afternoon had cleared up nicely. Soon the students would be back in town, the sand rinsed off their feet. Perhaps the girl would say, *we were chased by a seal,* and the boy would correct her, *it was a sea lion,* and then mother would say, *when I was young a rogue current pulled three girls out to sea there and they all drowned; it's a pity you were late, the casserole has all dried out;* and the boy would reply, *taste's fine to me, mum.* Then the young ones would look at each other, already in a hurry to get back to their flat, to the sagging line of washing, to the bed propped up on beer crates.

Hattie was in the middle of lacing her boots when an earthquake shook the windowpanes. Annoyed, she moved to stand in the doorway while she listened to the sea glass and the bones rattle on the shelves. *Go for higher ground,* the civil defence page in the back of the phone book said. *Don't go down to the sea to watch.* Hattie never paid any attention. Tsunami or not she would go down to sketch the dredge buckets before the light faded. Let any old tsunami take her; just let it roll her into the underwater fields. Wasn't the better part of her there already?

Scottish Annie

ON SATURDAYS AT FIVE Archie McLean visits the retirement home to take requests at the piano. Each week the seniors try to trip him. "Robins and Roses," they'll say, naming some old tune that they used to dance to on the wind-up. They can't catch Archie out. Archie knows them all and he sings in that old-fashioned radio way, leaning back on the piano stool, nodding to the ladies. At the end, he opens the piano lid right up and plays an extra fast bumblebee song. I'm usually out in the garden when Archie gets back after the tea and scones, and then he leans over the hedge to tell me about it.

"Well Ruby," says Archie, "I think we wowed them today." It always makes me laugh. You would think he was a whole orchestra the way he talks. Archie is a nice young man. Genteel, my mother would have said. We play Scrabble on Wednesday nights. He's been my neighbour for nearly fifteen years now. Back in March, he celebrated his fiftieth birthday, and I made an eggless chocolate cake, because Archie doesn't believe in exploiting the hens. He served me a slice and said, "so when's your birthday, Ruby?"

"Get away with you," I said, "a lady doesn't admit to her age until she's in for a telegram from the Queen. All I'm saying is I'm not old enough to be your mother. Have some more cake."

Last week, when he had finished toting up the score for the word *umbilical,* Archie told me that he has to move, because his landlord wants to sell the house. I was very sorry to hear that. Archie has been a great friend to me.

After mother died, three years ago next February, Archie got me started volunteering at the retirement home. He said it was better than hiding in the potting shed. At the time, I said that I wasn't hiding and that I'd think about it. Now I take the seniors out on wee trips in the car. Archie is the piano man and I am the driving jukebox. They tell me where they want to go, and I take them, within four hours and within reason. Often they like to go back to where they were born, or where they've had picnics in the past. One afternoon I drove ninety-year-old Willy Callaghan to Oamaru. We idled outside a renovated villa on Vine Street while Mr. Callaghan wept for the loss of the corrugated iron sheets on the roof and the front room where he had been born. I said that a nice conservatory full of tomatoes was nothing to cry about. Still, I let him have a good old weep, and then we went for an ice cream and came home. It takes me a year to get through all the seniors, so some of the older ones don't come more than once.

When I arrived up at the home last week, Mrs. Webster was waiting for me in the foyer, all wrapped up warm for her outing. She always wears mohair cardies that her niece from up Ranfurly way knits for her. The light catches in the hairs.

"You're glowing, Mrs. Webster," I said, and she was pleased. Mohair keeps your chest warm, but it's not cheap, and it gets stringy. Better to mix it with a bit of wool.

"Anyway," I said, "where are we off to today?" Mrs. Webster wanted to go to the nursery at Blueskin Bay, to buy a miniature rose for her bedroom. She had a coupon from the paper. They do love coupons. So off we went, out through Pine Hill and over the motorway to the nursery. She got a wee apricot rose to match her curtains. I almost got one too, but then I thought it was silly to get over-excited about plants that don't survive the winter.

Mrs. Webster was sitting in the car looking at the rose bush on her lap. Then she looked at me quite shyly.

"Do you think we could take the road along the coast, through Seacliff?" she asked.

"Of course we can, Mrs. Webster," I said. "My wish is your command." So away we went, winding along above the sea, past the rabbit holes in the yellow clay banks and the twisted macrocarpa trees along the fence lines.

"Seacliff always makes me sad," I said, just to make conversation. It's the kind of thing that people say when they drive through Seacliff. The paddocks there fall so steeply towards the sea that it's hard to tell how a sheep might hold on in the wind, let alone a farmer on a bike. And you think you might hear some ghost from the asylum wailing away in the breeze. It was a grand old place, the asylum at Seacliff, majestic and crenellated. They had proper lunatics in those days.

"Just here, Ruby dear, drive me up here," said Mrs. Webster, "up towards the asylum, to those trees at the top of the road." We stopped by a gate where there was nothing to see, just an old car with no headlights, buried in the bushes, and a pile of bricks to show where a house once stood.

"I was born here," said Mrs. Webster. "The back door faced the asylum, and the verandah ran all around the house. And up the hill under the eucalyptus trees there were passion fruit vines with purple flowers, all fringed with blue. Every year Mum would take us up to look at the flowers, and she would say, *See kids, even in Seacliff.* And we would say, *even in Seacliff what, Mum?* And she always replied, *even in Seacliff we can be on a tropical island.* She had a lovely laugh, our Mum."

"Shall we walk up and have a look Mrs. Webster?" I said. "Would you like that?" I helped her out of the car and into her coat, found her stick, took her arm. The wind was fierce. Together we took granny steps up the paddock towards the gum trees at the top.

"My mother was known as Scottish Annie," said Mrs. Webster. "She had that kind of bone-china skin that reddens in the southerly wind. She used to stand on the porch shading her eyes with her hand, looking out at the sea, while she sent my sister Milly to get the washing in, *quicksticks, before the rain comes.* It was a deal of work to keep the five of us washed and mended I can tell you. She did the washing on a Saturday, which was considered quite unusual, but that way the boys could help. Johnnie stirred the copper with a big stick. Our Mum didn't do things quite like other people."

Mrs. Webster was looking way out across the ocean. I could tell that she had a story to tell so I let her run. So many of the older ones only have fragments left, but that afternoon Mrs. Webster could still put her hand on the whole thing.

"Our Dad was killed by a coal dray coming down Stafford Street," said Mrs Webster. "Dad rolled right out of the pub and into the road and then the dray came clattering down the hill, and that was that. You might think that the coal merchant would have had the decency to send a load out to the widow, but he didn't.

"Mum let out the paddocks to Mr. Currie to run his cows on. The cows used to come up and look at us through the window. Then our Mum got a job serving hot dinner up at the asylum, but that still wasn't enough, so we got a lodger. His name was Mr. Reginald Hooper. Mr. Hooper was a clean-cut medical resident, neat as a pin, with round spectacles that he polished with a handkerchief that came out of his pocket, and such nice clean nails. He must have wondered what had happened to him, coming into our house with five kids roaring about. But he never said anything and he was as polite as you please, and out of the house early and not back until teatime. We had our tea first, and then Mum would give the lodger his stew and tell us to go away and let the man have his dinner in peace, because he worked in the madhouse all day and he didn't have to live in one too. We called him Mr. Hooper, but Johnnie sometimes called him Dr. Whooping Cough. We thought that was terribly funny.

"Mr. Hooper did his best to be handy about the house, even though Mum would never have asked him to lift a finger. A couple of the big eucalyptus trees up the back had been cut down and when Mr. Hooper came home in the evening he would chop his heart out with his sleeves rolled up and his dark hair flopping about. The first woodpile he made came down in the night. How we laughed. Mr. Hooper bit his lip and went out in the dark to stack it again. He liked to bring in a load and put it by the stove ready to use, and our Mum didn't have the heart to tell him that it would take six months to get the wood half-dry enough for burning.

"Mr. Hooper was nice to us kids too, and he didn't have to be. He brought in gum nuts and put them in a box for the baby to shake. And once, when he saw us watching him put his boots on, he turned his sock into a snake that spoke in a funny voice, and another time he did a shadow show on the wall with his hands—you know, the dove, the old woman, the Turk—all those shapes he could do.

"After dinner Mr. Hooper studied his medical books at the kitchen table. Our Mum sat in the cane chair with the sock basket on her knees, darning and watching him work. She made him a pot of tea, but she wouldn't take a cup herself. She was so proud to have Dr. Whooping Cough and his white coat staying at our house. She put him to sleep in the parlour! How people talked. It was cold in the front parlour. That's why Mr. Hooper studied his books in the kitchen.

"The four older kids, Frankie, Millie, Johnnie, and Meggie, went to school, but at the beginning, the baby went down the road to Mrs. Wren's. Then Mrs. Wren's back got bad and baby couldn't go there any more. So in the mornings, our Mum would put the baby in the pen containing the vegetable garden, plump down on its bottom among the cabbages. Every so often she would nip outside to shake out a rag and sing out tra-la-loo, just to check that the baby was alright. She must have been shaking out the rags every two minutes.

"One morning, while the older kids were at school and the baby was in the pen in the backyard, the kitchen chimney caught fire. All that resin from the green wood had built up in the dog-leg of the flue. Well, that's what Mr. Currie said later. He had warned our Mum, but the flue caught fire. It smouldered for a long time and then it got roaring hot. Our Mum had left her apron hung over the fire guard in the kitchen and the gum nuts in the pockets cracked open in the heat.

"Mr. Currie was on his way up the hill to look at Dolores who had hoof rot. He smelt the smoke and ran to the house. I saw the fire too, because I was that baby, you know. It's one of my earliest memories, poking a stick at a piece of wood where the paint has swelled up into lovely soft bubbles. Mr. Currie ran into the burning house and he found our Mum and the lodger passed out on the bed. Entwined they were. At noon. And her not even wearing a wrapper. Mr. Currie had to get it off the hook on the back of the door. First he brought our Mum out, and then Mr. Currie, such a brave man, went back in for Mr. Hooper. After that there was nothing that could be

155

done to save the house. Dry as tinder it was under the rafters. You must have been able to see the flames far out at sea.

"Mr. Currie laid Mum and Mr. Hooper side-by-side on the cold grass and covered them with a blanket. And the hill beside the house there is so steep that the bodies were almost standing up. Carbon monoxide had come creeping up on them. Well. They came round eventually. No harm done, and everyone said that it was a miracle. Even Mr. Currie said that, because if they had both died, who would have looked after all us kids?

"Well, Mr. Hooper did the decent thing, and he married our Mum, took her on with the five kids and even had another one. That's my younger brother Neil. He's up in the Ross Home now. And Mr. Hooper's parents, they also did the decent thing and they disowned him. And you can be sure that no one at Seacliff was going to let Scottish Annie have her cake and eat it too, dandling her young man in the bedroom while the house burned down and the baby sat in the backyard with The Lord Knows What in its mouth. So our Mum sold the paddocks and we all moved to Caversham, to a wee house in the shade of the hill. Mr. Hooper got work filling orders in a chemist's shop. But he would not let our Mum go to work, no he would not. She was his queen. Queen of the washboard, more like, but in those days, men were proud and they didn't want their women to work.

"For a long time, we had nothing at all, except swedes, boiled and mashed and roasted. My stepfather was a good man. I never saw his belt buckle coming my way and that's a lot more than the older ones could say for our Dad. Mr. Hooper was the only Dad I ever knew. So, it's not just sorrow that comes out of Seacliff. It was good for us kids, at any rate until the war came. But that wasn't just us. That was everybody."

By the time she finished talking, Mrs. Webster and I were back in the car, fussing with the seatbelts, trying to get our hands warm. Heading back into town, I wanted to say to her, but you were the baby – if you can't remember the bodies laid out on the grass and the passion-fruit flower sitting in a cup of water on the kitchen table, then how do you know that it happened that way? But the story was true. Mrs. Webster knew it by heart. You could tell. And I could not bother her with questions, because she had fallen asleep. That's how it is with these trips in the car. Clear as a bell, like a song in all its verses, and then their eyelids come down and the story is finished.

I don't mind letting on that I envied Mrs. Webster her story. I would have liked a large family and a life rounded out with pots of tea, biscuits and chat at the kitchen table. Mother always said that I could not expect much with my blunt features and heavy bones. Not that any of it matters now, at my age, no matter what the magazines say.

Still, I have a good mind to ask Archie if he would like to take the granny flat at the bottom of the garden. It has a brand new refrigerator that never saw more than a bottle of milk because Mother took all her meals with me. I rather fancy the sound of the piano coming up from behind the buddleia. He could have the folding card table and Mother's extra chairs. We could make tea and play Scrabble on Wednesday nights. He could be a proper lodger.

Oh I know you're thinking that I'm after Archie, but you'd be wrong, for Archie McLean is not the marrying kind. No, it's just that after I've passed on, I'd rather like it if one person, and maybe it might be Archie, would stop the car outside my bungalow, smile at the upturned faces of the marigolds, and say, yes, happy times we had there, happy times.

Acknowledgements

First of all, a big thank you to Dan Wells, John Metcalf and the team at Biblioasis for giving this collection a home between covers. Thank you for your time and your dedication.

During the last five years I have benefited from the mentorship of two astute critics: Sandra Birdsell of the Humber College programme for writers and Ami Sands-Brodoff of the Quebec Writers' Federation, assisted by a grant from the Canada Council for the Arts. Sandra, Ami, please accept my thanks for helping to make this a better book. I have also had much support from family and friends in New Zealand, Canada and the USA. I would like to thank in particular Sarah Winters, my ideal reader, and my husband Gary Duncan.

The Elcarim recipe in "Where the Corpse Weed Grows" is based on the formula Essiac, developed in the 1930s by Nurse René Caisse, after an Ojibway herbal medicine.

I would also like to acknowledge the inspiration of chef Marie-Christine Potvin and her recipe *Perchaude aux trois agrumes et ses avocats frits* (copyright Académie Culinaire de Montréal). The garlic is my own ill-advised addition, since this is fiction after all.

Some of these stories have been previously published: "After Summer," *Geist 62*, 2006, *Journey Prize Stories*, 19 (McLelland & Stewart, 2007), *Coming Attractions 08* (Oberon Press); "Vandals in Sandals," *Short Stuff: New English Writing in Quebec* (Véhicule Press, 2005); "Neither Up Nor Down," *Takahe 56*, 2005; "Salsa Madre," *Geist 69*, 2008, *Coming Attractions 08* (Oberon Press, 2008); "Among the Trees" *Coming Attractions 08* (Oberon Press, 2008), *The Fiddlehead 240*, 2009; "Scottish Annie," *The Fiddlehead, 237*, 2008; "The Land Below," *Room 32.3*, 2009; "Through the Gates," *Takahe 70*, 2010, "Neptune's Necklace," *Fiddlehead 248*, 2011.

Soon after I arrived in Canada in the autumn of 1994, Ruth and Kenneth Perkins introduced me to the pleasures of lake-side living on the Canadian Shield. I will always be grateful for their welcome and special care. This book is dedicated to Ken's memory: finest of musicians, kindest of friends.

GARY DUNCAN

New Zealander-Canadian Alice Petersen was the 2009 winner of the David Adams Richards Award, offered by the Writers' Federation of New Brunswick. Her stories, published in *Geist, The Fiddlehead, Room,* and *Takahe,* have variously been shortlisted for the Journey Prize, the Writers' Union of Canada competition, the CBC Literary awards, and the Metcalf-Rooke Award. Petersen lives in Montreal with her husband and two daughters. *All the Voices Cry* is her first collection.